MAN OF BONE

Man of Bone

A NOVEL

ALAN CUMYN

To Cynthia Keppley Mahmood,

With gratitude,

Alan R. Cumyn

April 1998

First Edition

GOOSE LANE

Published by Goose Lane Editions with the assistance of the Canada Council, the Department of Canadian Heritage, and the New Brunswick Department of Municipalities, Culture and Housing, 1998.

This novel is a work of fiction. Names, characters, places and incidents are the product of the author's imagination, and their resemblance, if any, to real-life counterparts is entirely coincidental. Some sections from this novel, in different form, first appeared in *Blood & Aphorisms* ("Dance," fall 1996) and *The Pottersfield Portfolio* ("Maryse's Apartment," summer 1997). The author gratefully acknowledges the financial assistance of the Canada Council in the preparation of this manuscript. Thanks, too, to the staff at the Centre for Victims of Torture in Toronto for taking the time to discuss aspects of their work, and to the many friends, family members and colleagues whose comments, suggestions and support have been invaluable. Finally, thanks to Laurel Boone for her editorial hand and encouragement. The deficiencies that remain are entirely mine. A.C.

Edited by Laurel Boone.
Cover photograph by Dale McBride.
Cover and interior design by Julie Scriver.
Printed in Canada by Transcontinental Printing.

10   9   8   7   6   5   4   3   2   1

Canadian Cataloguing in Publication Data

Cumyn, Alan, 1960-
    Man of Bone
    ISBN 0-86492-146-2

1. Title.

PS8555.U489M36 1998   C813' .54   C98-950070-5
PR9199.3.C775M36 1998

Goose Lane Editions
469 King Street
Fredericton, New Brunswick
CANADA E3B 1E5

To those who work to hasten the dawn

Black oil pit. Hands out to each side but there's no wall. No wall, no tree, no door, nothing solid. Just black, oily air. Can't move my head to see. I open my eyes but see only blackness. Take a step, can't keep my balance but don't fall either. Try to drop to my knees, crawl, feel something with my hands but can't, something holds me up. Try to yell but my voice won't work. No sound, just the smell of the oily black air. Have to hurry because of the noise from behind, don't know what it is, have to move move move or it'll get me. But where? Trying to run in slow motion, then stepping on snakes, a mass of them, try to pull out but it's too late, they bite at my leg, can't see them, pain shoots through me. Shake, thrash, try to cry out but there's no voice, hands can't move to rip them off. Writhe in panic, and they bite now up my calves, my thighs, tear now at my testicles, but my hands won't move to get them off. Tremble, scream, roll, no escape just oily black air . . .

Awake. Now I'm awake, heart pounding, shit — awake. No snakes. There aren't any snakes. The blackness is the hood, the oily smell from the many layers of paint that keep out all light. My shackled legs. The needles of pain from this cramped position against the wall and floor — those were the snakes. Wet and cold, which is the night; hot like an oven would be day. I try to move my fingers. My arms are strapped behind my back but I can't feel them anymore. Neck and shoulders in constant pain, feet and legs too, but my arms have no feeling at all. I'm seized with the thought that I've lost them, they've been amputated. I rock back and forth. Something under my bum, a straw mat or my fingers. I try to breathe slowly, not give in to the panic. Mat? Fingers? Everything's in pain, but what wouldn't I give for pain in my fingers to show they're still there? Please God, I think, please God, whoever you are, please God, give me pain in my fingers!

Nothing. I stop rocking, slow my breathing. It's hard enough in this damn hood, the mouth hole just big enough to keep me alive. Message from brain: Fingers, can you read me? Fingers, do you copy? Fingers, if you copy, give me a sign. Move, fingers. Scratch the floor. Scratch your bum. Fingers. Just flex. Fingers, if you can read me . . .

There's no time. I'm in the no-time place. Stay awake. Brain to body: Stay awake! Brain to brain: No more sleeping. There are snakes in that sleep, snakes or worse. Stay alert. APB: All units will stay awake for five minutes. Brain will count out the time. Five minutes. One steamboat, two steamboat, three steamboat. Reminder: All units on red alert for the next five minutes. Six steamboat, seven steamboat. Fingers, if you hear me, fingers, work on flexing. You were coming along. The message is on its way. When your receiver is back on-line: Flex. Fingers, do you copy? Ten steamboat, eleven . . .

A sound. Everything stops. Steamboats, fingers, breathing. Stops for the sound. In the oily world, hot now, daytime. What day? Two or three. Monday, I think. Because Friday was badminton at Kaireen. I don't think I got there. I remember driving, trying to get out of the city. I don't remember the badminton. It's hard to remember anything but oil and blackness.

The sound is traffic. Traffic is nearby. I'm in a closet somewhere, or a basement, and the street is close, I can hear it. Engines. Everything is muffled but I think it's engines. I think there are voices but I can't make out any words.

Brain to brain: What happened to the steamboats? You were going to count off five minutes and think of nothing else. A mental exercise. Stay awake for five minutes. It's hard with the oiliness coming in and out. I have to keep my head up. If I let it fall forward then the hood starts to choke me. It must be fastened to the wall. I'm shackled and handcuffed and hooded. If I still have hands, that is. I do, I know I do. They just aren't responding. If they'd amputated them I'd be in a whole lot more pain. I wouldn't even be alive.

Maybe I'm not alive?

Maybe I'm *not* alive. I'm dead. I was driving to Kaireen but there was trouble which I can't remember, and now this is hell. I'm in hell. Hell is being shackled and hooded and handcuffed in a closet or basement or wherever this is and freezing at night and roasting in the day and smelling shit and piss from your own pants.

Brain to brain: How many steamboats? This is a Zen trick: Focus yourself. No stray thoughts for five minutes. Not even in hell. Not even if you're dead. Twelve steamboats, thirteen steamboats, fourteen steamboats, fifteen steamboats.

Five minutes will be five times sixty steamboats which is three hundred. Sixteen steamboats. Brain to brain: Keep counting!

Why can't I smell my shit and piss? I could before. That wasn't a dream. The first time I had to go, I held it and held it and yelled for someone, but there was no one, and then finally the release, the warm, unstoppable spreading, and then the cold and the smell and disgust. I didn't dream that. It was real. Why can't I smell it now? I'm getting so numb, but I'd know if there was shit in my pants. I'd know it but I can't feel it.

Brain to fingers: Come in, fingers! Flex, damn it!

Maybe someone has cleaned me. When I was asleep. I should

feel hungry but I don't. If I've been here three days then why don't I feel hungry? I'm twisted and wrecked. I can't remember eating.

I can't remember eating but now that I think of it I'm starving. Blink my eyes in oily blackness and I'm not sure anything happened, but if I work my jaw I know. What do I know? I'm here, I'm starving, my mouth is dry, every breath parches me even more, scratches down my throat. Water! God, please, water! I try to make my voice work but it won't. People are walking somewhere a wall away and I can't even make my voice work!

I need a plan. I need to know what to do. I have to get out of here. Someone has grabbed me. It's one of the Kartouf groups, one of the factions, but which one? There's over a hundred. Why didn't I learn about the bloody factions? Factions was next week. You got me too soon. I followed the goddamn safe route!

There — how do I know that? That was a memory. My mind is waking up. Brain to brain: Good work. You were on the safe route. You followed the map. Then what? Then what? I don't think I got to Kaireen. Something must've happened. Brain to brain: What about those steamboats?

Maryse wasn't in the car with me. Where was she? She was going to Kaireen but she wasn't in the car. She was getting a ride with Marlene the Australian vegetarian.

Why didn't *anybody* say anything about the factions? One of them has me and I've got to get out. To hell with the steamboats. I'm not going to be able to move much longer. I'm going to be a vegetable.

I *am* a vegetable.

I can't move. I can't move a finger. My legs are sticks of pain that turn to fire when I try to move, and when I lean forward this damn hood chokes me, and as far as I know I don't have any arms left, and I'm chained and shackled. I'm going nowhere.

Don't panic. Emergency Situations: Insurrection, sitting beside Williams in that sleep-sealed lecture hall. *Don't panic.* That's the key. Panic makes things worse. If they were going to kill you they would've done it at the beginning. The longer you stay alive, the better your chances.

I'm still alive. My chances are good. My chances are fair. I have a chance still. I don't know who I'm dealing with. I don't even know if there's shit in my pants. I've not been briefed for this. Williams, do you hear me? I've not been briefed!

Joke. That was a joke. The international signal: Raise your left hand when you're making a joke. Only I'm not sure I have a left hand. I can't see it. I can't feel it. The tree just fell in the middle of the goddamn forest!

Williams is in Bangkok now on his first posting. He gets Bangkok, I get Santa Irene. Who ever heard of it?

If you can't take a joke, why'd you sign up?

All right, all right, heart — slow. *Three weeks into his first posting, young Burridge gets kidnapped driving to badminton.* That seems to be the situation. "Hi Mom. Yes, it's Bill. It's a clear line, isn't it? Just like I'm in the next room. How are things? Good, Mom, things are good. They're fine, they're just . . .well, there's some cross-cultural stuff to get used to. Well, you know, just little stuff, like, when you get kidnapped by one of the factions. Yes, that's what I said. I mean, it's a good idea to know *which faction you're dealing with.* It's, like, one of those basic things. The cutbacks, you know, we don't get briefed as well as we could. Like, you have to wait four weeks before you get factions training, so if you get kidnapped in the first *three* weeks . . . but, of course, it wouldn't happen, I'm talking hypothetically here. You wouldn't get kidnapped in your first three weeks because, first of all, you don't know anything, so why would someone kidnap you, and second of all, they give you this map, Mom, and on the map are these *safe zones*, they're all marked out in green. Green for *go*, you see. Those are the roads where it's safe. Because the government troops are everywhere on those green roads, and the factions, they couldn't touch you even if they wanted to. I mean, they'd have to bribe their way in, you see, Mom, and this is Santa Irene, there's no *way* a Kartouf faction could just bribe their way past an army check-point. Those soldiers, I mean, they get thirteen dollars, hey, fifteen dollars a month. They're *impervious* to bribes. I mean, *Safety* comes with a capital *S* here on Santa Irene. So don't worry about Bill. Good heavens, no. I'd hang up the phone, Mom, but I'm not sure which hand I'm holding it in . . ."

Dial 911. That's the answer. From that team-building exercise with Henry and Loretta and what's-his-name from Vancouver. Stuck in the mountains after the plane crash, you have eighteen items but can take only ten, which ones and in what order? Para-chute silk and aluminum foil and matches . . . Henry, his face red from drinking all night, bursts in, "Hey, why don't we just dial 911?" Why was that funny at the time? It was hilarious. Dial 911.

Another sound and my heart hammers against my ribs. Not just traffic. A door. Footsteps. Heavy boots. Suddenly I feel my fingers, just like that, like they've been held on the burner, *God!* and then hands pull me out, my legs flaming in the pain of the movement, my neck jerked, screaming my throat raw. Pushed, I fall forward, but my hood doesn't choke me, they must've released it. Then white pain from my eyes when they grab off the hood, I close them but it's still white, blinding. I turn my head but there's no escape, cruel whiteness everywhere.

"Still!" yells someone, and he follows up with a boot to my ribs and then a long stream of Kuantij. "I can't I don't I'm sorry I don't understand," I say, but my voice is a whisper and it's hard to make the words come out properly. I'm searching for a phrase but my brain is in a panic.

"Please I'm sorry please I don't I can't please I can't." Feeble. My body shaking, everything's on fire, he's going to kick me again I know I know I know. Whiteness everywhere.

But it gets still.

There's more than one of them. Suddenly I can hear a whole rush of breathing, like there's an army of them nearby. I can't see a thing. It's too bright.

"Water, please," I say, opening my mouth and feeling the flesh tear at the corners. How to say it? *"Lojo, japeh!"*

Quiet. I'm broken on the floor. Oh, my limbs! How long was I bolted to the wall? God, just stretching my leg makes it feel bent against the hinge.

"Lojo, japeh!" I can't pronounce the words. There's a way to say the *j* so that it sounds like the rush of a waterfall, and then another way so that it sounds like a glassy smooth lake at dawn.

Silence, silence. The whiteness worse and worse. Are they shining some kind of high beam right at my face? It's not up to me to say anything here. Gentlemen, you're the ones who called this meeting. If you don't have anyone who speaks English then we'll never understand each other.

Silence, I can't stand it. They're all breathing, breathing, looking at me. Someone's smoking. Not saying a word.

"I can't talk," I whisper, my mouth pointed down into the concrete floor, which feels cool. Is this nighttime? "I need water — *lojo, lojo, japeh!* Please, if you want me to say something you have to bring me water."

I wait. They just look and breathe.

But I can't look. It's as if they've pried off the top of my skull and are shining a laser down my cortex. There's no escape, no way to move.

Just looking and breathing. The cigarette gets closer. The whole room seems full of smoke now, it's hard to get air, mouth and nose against the filthy floor. Then I know what they're going to do. They're going to take their cigarettes and burn my skin. "No!" I say and try to crawl but it hurts too much.

"Still!" That voice comes again and then hands press on me and I know they're going to burn me. I cry out and try to turn, but they hold me down and then I feel the needle jabbed into my thigh and scream until my mouth cracks.

"There's no wind here," Maryse says. She's holding a badminton racket but isn't wearing any clothes and her skin is glowing and brown. I mean to ask her how her skin got so brown when she burns in the faintest sun. But she looks gorgeous this way, too, her hair braided with tropical flowers and her nipples chocolate.

"That's why they're such good badminton players," Maryse says. "There's no wind. So they can play anywhere."

"So you got to Kaireen all right? With the vegetarian lesbian?"

"Marlene. She's not a lesbian. She's Australian and vegetarian, but she's not a lesbian."

"And Patrick is okay?"

Maryse looks down.

"I mean — Patrick is all right. They didn't get Patrick. They got me, but they didn't get Patrick."

Maryse looks up. "It's because there isn't any wind. It's a natural advantage. Like ice in winter for hockey."

"Where's Patrick?" I scream. "They didn't get him, right?"

"It's an island, but there isn't any wind."

"Patrick!" I try to run to him and it's an island so there's no wind, just a fucking typhoon, it blows me off my feet and I'm twisted twisted twisted. I think I see him, twisting somewhere else in the wind and rain. "Patrick! Patrick!" He's too little, he can't hear me. "Patrick!"

Someone has hammered a spike into my skull. I open my eyes to oily blackness, and when I lean forward the choke rope grabs my neck so I know I'm back on the wall, still here. But everything is dull and slow. They didn't get Patrick. They didn't get Maryse. Maryse isn't brown-skinned. They got me, and I'm here and broken. I can smell the shit again. But it isn't shit. I've vomited in the hood. It's all around my mouth, caked, rotting personal sewage.

And a spike running down the back of my brain. Maryse — you and your migraines.

Now I know.

You just want to die. To get it over.

There isn't an ounce of fight left.

Why am I here?

I just am.

Breathing my own vomit. In this moment. No way to move. More sleep. There might be escape in more sleep. How do I sleep? I sleep when the needle comes into me. When the cigarettes come closer and closer and the voice says, "Still!" I get still, become a puddle in the bottom of a hole. And when the sleep comes it's all right at first. It isn't this everything-broken feeling, this spike in my skull, this hundred years of aging dumped on me.

Sleep is somewhere else. I wait for the cigarettes, wait for the voice, "Still!" and then I know it'll be all right. Sometimes in the sleep they take Patrick and Maryse but that's just sleep, it isn't real. Real is chained against the wall, hooded in my own vomit. Real is my body rotting.

I must be going insane. My body's broken and soon my brain will be, too. Brain to brain: Do some steamboats. One steamboat two. But what if the cigarettes won't come? If they hear my steamboats they won't come and there won't be the needle. Maybe they can't hear the steamboats but maybe they can and if they can they won't come because they'll know I'm still trying to resist. I'm not trying to resist. I'm a puddle at the bottom of a hole. Bring the needle!

Bring the needle. Bring the needle. I'll think of that for five minutes. I'll say to myself "bring the needle" three hundred times and then it'll come. First there'll be the cigarettes and then maybe bright whiteness, and sometimes they kick me, but in the end it's worth it because they bring the needle. Bring the needle, bring the needle, bring the needle. They think they've captured me, but when they bring the needle then that's when I can escape. It's my one chance. I might end up in a typhoon chasing after Patrick but I might escape too. It's possible. Chained, broken, hooded in my own vomit — I'm just a puddle at the bottom of a hole. But after the needle . . .

Bring the needle, bring the needle, bring the needle. Bring the needle one, bring the needle two, bring the needle three . . . please listen, I'm sending out these thoughts. Bring the needle four, bring the needle five. When I get to three hundred then they'll bring the needle. Bring the needle six.

They didn't really get Maryse and Patrick. I know they didn't. I can't remember how I know but I know. I know it for a fact. *For a fact.* Who used to always say that? Somebody did. The voice is in my head right now. *I know that for a fact young man . . .*

Dad. Of course. I know that. I know it for a fact. When someone presses his buttons he says it. There's a picture of him in my mind, suddenly angry, leaning across the dining room table. What's he angry about? There's something he knows for a fact. I can't remember what. What does he know? Something I said got him angry. It was about Cuba. He's such an American about Cuba.

"I know for a fact that Castro is running a totalitarian Communist regime, and if you deal with these people instead of making them pariahs then you suffer for it again and again. A Hitler doesn't go away, he just keeps knocking down your doors till you shut him up."

"Oh, come on, Dad, Castro's no Hitler. We're not contributing to the Holocaust by trading with Cuba. It's the American embargo that's practically starving people. Canada has — "

"Canada has shit for brains about Cuba! I know for a fact . . ."

No, Dad, I don't want to listen. This isn't the time. This won't make things better. Bring the needle, bring the needle, bring the needle. How many was that? Ten. Bring the needle eleven. Bring the needle twelve. When I get to three hundred the needle will be here. First come the cigarettes, then the whiteness and the boots, but not for long, not for too long. If I just stay a puddle I can manipulate them. They don't know what to do with a puddle. They just bring the needle and that's my escape.

Bring the needle thirteen, bring the needle fourteen. That old stuff, that *I know for a fact* business, Dad, everybody from out there, that's over. It's part of another universe. I've gone to another universe. It's different here. It's all changed.

So I'm dead already. I know it suddenly. I'm dead and back in a womb of sorts, getting ready to be born again. It isn't comfortable at all, it's bloody cramped, and you breathe your own vomit, and the only escape is sleep and dreaming. There are awful things in dreams but good things, too. Maryse with brown skin and chocolate nipples. Maybe she'll be my wife in the next life. Maybe I'll have brown skin. Maybe I've died on Santa Irene and so this is where I'll be re-born, so of course I'll have brown skin.

Bring the needle, bring the needle, bring the needle. Playing prisoner with Davy Littlejohn and what was his name, that kid with the blond curly hair? What was his name? "Vee haf vays to make you talk!" Tied up with string behind the garage, poking your belly with sticks. "Careful! Watch my eye, you moron!" "Silence! Vee haf vays!"

It isn't like that. It's not like that. They don't even talk to you. I don't think they have anyone who speaks English. The Kartouf, they think they're the centre of the bloody universe, of course everyone would speak Kuantij.

Bring the needle. Please bring the needle! If you aren't going to feed me. You've puddled my body, just bring the needle! I'd tell you anything, I would, but I don't know a thing!

Seventeen. Bring the needle eighteen. When I get to forty they'll bring the needle. I can't get to three hundred. But when I get to forty . . .

I don't care if it's snakes. Once it was cancer. I was in my bed and could see the doctors scraping it out of my chest. It looked like gravel. I thought it would be grey but light, not heavy, not gravel. Scraping it out. It looked as if they were going to use a shovel. I was shrieking, every shovelful was real, real. I couldn't move, couldn't look away, and the pain turned my bones to chalk. I woke up and my bones were chalk, I was gravel inside, being taken away one shovelful at a time.

But I still need the needle.

If they asked me anything I'd tell them. But they don't ask. They just have me. They're killing me slowly. Faster would be better, a bullet to the brain. They must have guns, factions generally have guns. How do I know that? Most factions have guns. I know it for a fact. A bullet to the brain and then I'd have a lot more sleep but it wouldn't be cancer sleep. They wouldn't pull gravel out of my chest. There wouldn't be snakes, it would be grey sleep, black sleep, no-thought sleep. How could I think without a brain?

They didn't get Patrick or Maryse. They're safe. They're back in Canada now. The department is looking after them. As soon as they know I'm dead the house is paid for, the insurance kicks in, Maryse, you're a full-time painter. Patrick's university is paid. The best thing Burridge did his whole life. Took a bullet to the brain. Everything worked out after that.

Bring the needle, bring the bullet, bring the needle, either one. I'm dead anyway. I'm back in the womb and it feels like shit. Like my body's been cracked and broken and repacked and I just have to get smaller and smaller. Reverse birth. Cells have to de-divide. Regress to the fetus.

That's my job now. To become Patrick. I can't do it without the needle. Needle or the bullet. Footsteps, cigarettes, the boot. Please come. Please come! Bring the needle. Bring the bullet. Shoot right into my brain. Either one. I'm on a reverse birth anyway. Reverse birth is death. I have to get small enough. I'm too big for this space. I can't do it alone. Please come!

They don't come. I count, wait, pray, but they don't come. They're listening. They know. They know so they don't come.

"Boo-reej! Like something eed, no?"

The thin man laughs. He has a face like the blade of a wedge. Black eyebrows sloping back. Mustache too, like a chevron. When he smiles his teeth show white like exposed bone.

I look down, wait to fly. I lift one foot and then the other and as I step I'm leaping easily, hovering like on a moonwalk, but my feet don't come down, so really I'm flying. I look down, wait for the feeling, but this is a different dream.

"Porridge."

"Wha?"

"Something to eat. Porridge."

"Is that wan, burridge?" I see him through cigarette smoke. Very brown eyes, almost black. Not the colour so much as the shadows. Maryse could do those shadows. But she's from before. She doesn't belong to this life. There's no needle with Maryse.

I'm still waiting to fly.

"Wan burridge?" the man asks. "Is wan?"

I want to say yes but the words won't come out.

"Ged too theen." He's thin himself, but his skin is brown and shines like oiled wood so he looks luxurious, strong. "We wan find you can eed."

"No. No." Eating is impossible. How can I eat and fit back into the dark place? Eating makes everything more painful. "Needle."

"Lader. You aren care yoursel."

His voice like oil on wood. His skin and his voice. Warm and smooth. Someone yelled at me before. This man isn't yelling. He hasn't kicked me yet. It doesn't matter. I'm close now to where kicking doesn't reach.

"Meg burridge, or Merica. Fried chicken, steg? You to tell us. Must you eed."

I shake my head. He's not all whiteness like the others. I can see him. So this must be a dream. But my body feels broken like sticks in a bag, and I want the needle still so how can it be a dream? I want the needle, which means I'm not dreaming, but how can I see him if I'm not dreaming?

"I like brown sugar."

"Brawn sugra?"

"On my porridge."

He nods as if he's going to get up and fetch some for me. But he doesn't move.

"And milk."

"Melg."

"Brown sugar and milk." When I say the words I'm ravenous for it, can feel the sweetness and the warmth in my mouth. I must have it. It hurts so much not to have it. It hurts so much but how can it hurt when I'm just broken sticks? I can't even lift my head. I'm lying on the floor looking up. How did I get here?

"Thad wha feed you C-I-A, brawn sugra melg? Thad wha men eed Merica?"

His boot is close to my face so even though he isn't yelling he could kick me. I see this as if I'm watching from a distance. Almost out of reach. Before when they kicked me and yelled I was frightened and cried and shrieked and tried to crawl, but there was no way to escape. I just hurt and hurt and hurt. Everything they did hurt except the needle. But now I'm almost past where they can hurt. His boot is close to my face but it doesn't matter because my face is mushed like mud anyway. More boots in the face wouldn't matter. But I mustn't eat. That will only make it bad again.

"Thad C-I-A men eed — brawn sugra burridge?"

His voice soft like a gentle dentist's but I sense the whir of the drill in the background.

"I doun wan let otherz bek," he says. His cigarette is right beside my face. I can smell the oil on his skin. His cigarette is close enough to burn but it wouldn't. I'm not shaking.

"Member otherz?"

As soon as he says it I remember them. He's put them right in my head. With the others it's blackness or whiteness and then shrieking.

"Member?"

"Yes." It's like razors inside my throat to say it.

"Whad they do?"

As soon as he says it they're there with the black box like a car battery and the wires, and I'm shaking like lightning is after me.

"Whad they do. I wan stopping them, but they — well, cawboyz. You know where they tach it, those cawboyz?"

I'm shock-frozen.

"Nut caizis!" he says, his eyes gentle through the smoke. "They wan see is C-I-A diffren I-S."

I'm not CIA. And I'm not Santa Irenian Intelligence Service. I turn my head and try to say I don't know anything. I'm a Canadian Immigration Officer. If I could just tell him then they'd know. But words are hard. Words won't come out.

"I-S see box, shit like wimmen. You should see. Offsirrs wurzd. Die in part an hour they so fear. British bring box furzd. They copy it. Now beg keeled. Not like Kartouf. Doun got cyanide. Doun care wha to doing."

His voice becomes smoke soon. I try to make sense of the words but they're hard to grasp. I can't stay awake. I sleep and sleep but I'm so tired. I'm going back to the womb. That's my job now. Becoming Patrick. Cyanide would be good. Why don't I have cyanide? In a capsule around my neck. Like the Kartouf. There, I do know something about the Kartouf. They blow people up by strapping plastic explosives to their bodies and wear cyanide on leather necklaces. Like the Tamil Tigers.

"Lissn!" He grabs my face, forcing my eyes open.

Listen to what? Why doesn't he just kill me? I'd be glad to go. They could take their shovels out of my ribcage and there'd be no more gravel.

"Lissn!" he hisses again. I can't keep my eyes open, won't. He squeezes my face with hands hard as stones. "I-S men hurd Kartouf wurzed. Women childrenz cut killed slow. Box and box and scream women childrenz front your eyz. Cut belly baby. My childrenz! Wife and childrenz." He unbuttons his shirt and forces my eyes to his skin, black and bubbled like charcoal.

"Kartouf barbecue. Lissn!"

His eyes are black water and I don't want to see what they've seen.

"I applied for Beijing. You know I've geared everything for Beijing."

I'm standing in Marcia Coleman's office, the paper in my hand. She's in her red tailored executive suit. Her face is puffy about something, I don't know why and I don't care. I was supposed to get Beijing. It was just a formality.

"Bill, I'm sorry, you know that for first postings there are no promises."

"I went to Beijing with Khoury and he said he liked my work! You know I've been doing the language classes."

She stands now behind her desk, her hands flat. Nails chewed short — it's an odd detail, because everything else is immaculate:

her hair swooped back behind one ear, her gold buttons matching her hoop earrings and bracelet, the red of her suit and her shoes and her lipstick, each eyebrow a perfect arch. She'd be attractive if she didn't look like a museum display.

I'm livid, clutching my paper. "I don't even know where Santa Irene is!"

"It's in the South China Sea," she says. "Between Vietnam and —"

"I can find it, thank you!"

She purses her lips as if ready to deliver a verbal blow. I don't want to wait for it. This is such a disappointment. I was *geared* for Beijing.

And then she's crying. Just like that. Tough bureaucrat one moment, weeping woman the next.

"Oh, Marcia, what?"

Confusion. I step toward her but I don't really know her well enough to put my arm around her. Besides, she's my personnel officer.

"Nu-uthing." Her lips catch on empty syllables, her perfect makeup now streaked with tears.

She turns to open her bottom drawer and pulls out a tissue from the box there in one familiar movement, as if she has been doing this all day. In a moment she has wiped herself and seems composed once again.

"Uh, is there anything I can . . ."

"What they say in the department about this sort of thing, Bill, is if you can't take a joke, why'd you sign up?"

After I leave I ask the clerk, Janine, what's wrong with Marcia.

"Rosemary has leukemia," she says.

"Rosemary?"

"Her little girl."

No water today, but something else, clear and runny, like weak bitter jelly. Wedge Face tried to tell me what it is but all I understand is it's made from trees and for half the island people this is their only food. One of my eyes blinks and tears uncontrollably so I see through a strobe light. I'm cold, too, my limbs shake with it, I can't generate enough heat. I don't want to eat but the spoon keeps going into my mouth and I can't turn away, something is holding my head.

Holding my head and making my mouth fall open. I can't remember anything before this and don't want to know anything after. It's as if I've been swimming in darkness and suddenly, unaccountably, have burst through the surface into a present I can hardly recognize. But here I am, achingly here, gasping for this food like it's air.

They pretend to kill people. I don't know why I know this. They put prisoners through mock executions. They take off their hoods and line them up against the wall and draw their guns, then fire to miss, and the prisoners dissolve in terror. It's one more way they destroy you but keep you alive. I chew on wood jelly and shake with cold and watch Wedge Face through a nervous strobe, and this thought comes through like a commandment: The Kartouf destroy you but keep you alive.

It feels like the first clear thought I've ever had in my life. They destroy you but keep you alive. You want to die but you can't. You can't remain yourself but you can't die either. There's nothing you can do. You think they're killing you but they aren't.

The spoon keeps coming but I can't keep up. It's attached to a hand in space that belongs to someone else. Not Wedge Face. He's sitting across from me. There's a table in the room. One high window, with painted canvas over it. Probably we're still in a basement. There are three fluorescent lights. One of them works. There's a spider in the corner about the size of my hand. I can see it clearly despite the strobe light.

The spoon knocks my mouth because I haven't kept up and

then something rattles on the table and I look down. It's an entire tooth, yellow and brown. It spins a moment then stops.

I run my tongue through the new gap. The wood jelly comes out of my mouth and washes down my lips and cheeks like I'm coughing up Pablum. Wedge Face doesn't react. The spoon and its hand go away. There's no door in the room. Either it's behind me or this isn't really a room.

Sometimes it's not really a room. Sometimes if I wait it all goes away.

Which is what I'll do when they come to kill me. I'll wait and then it'll all go away. I'm not myself anymore but they won't kill me either. Like in the movies when you know the good guys aren't going to get it. No matter what happens.

No matter how much you want to die you can't. There's no escape.

They've screwed up on the needle, got careless, missed the vein. So I'm in the trunk of a car but still awake. It's nighttime, I think, but hard to tell because of the hood. I can smell the dust of the road. My head keeps bumping against something hard, a tire iron or a shovel blade. The noise is terrible. It's so hard to breathe, and I'm so angry. I want the needle when they move me. I don't need to be awake for this shit.

Josef told me every time I get the needle some Kartouf children have to go without food, that's how expensive it is. Josef is Wedge Face. He's the only one I recognize. The others are violent blanks in the shut-down part of my brain. I don't want to think about them. Just about Josef. Because he keeps the others from hurting me too much. They want to pull me to pieces, dump me in plastic bags in front of the CIA headquarters on Cardinal Avenue.

Josef says he knows now I'm not CIA but the others don't believe it yet. So he's keeping me alive. He tries to get me the needle but sometimes he can't.

His skin was burned by the IS. He was just a plantation worker, but one day he was on the wrong bus and got pulled off at a checkpoint for not having identification. Two others who were with him were shot and left in a ditch. Josef was taken to an interrogation centre and burned till he could smell his own flesh cooking. Then he was thrown out of the back of a police van. He rolled and rolled on the dirt, then he blacked out.

It was the Kartouf who found him, brought him to one of their hospitals in the mountains, nursed him back to health. Trained him to fight. His wife and children were burned along with most of the others from his village. The rest of his life he owes to the Kartouf. And that's the way all of the fighters feel. The IS, the army, the president, the whole *lumito* — the two-percent platinum-lined class that own everything on this island — they have to be wiped away because they won't give up any of it. The tinted glass in their limousines doesn't even allow them to see the children dying in the streets. Their news cameras capture nothing of life in Welanto, the fly-infested shantytown growing like a swamp around the capital. The Kartouf was born in Welanto, grew there like a disease, then spread to the mountains and the jungles where it became undefeatable.

Suffering is at the heart of it. Everyone who's part of the Kartouf has suffered. That's why I'm breathing dust in the trunk of this car, speeding to another prison. Josef wants to show the others that they don't have to kill me. That I can be useful.

But I have to suffer. There's no way around it.

Thoughts. Most of the time like bad soup, greasy, slopping, murky and aimless. With the needle they're like that. Without the needle, most of the time, they're radiator fluid in my brain, leaving me shaking with fear and disgust. Knowing what they've done. What they can and will do.

Josef comes with the clear wood jelly — he calls it *linala*. It seems just once a day but I can't tell. I'm outside time, like a space traveller going too fast and nowhere at the same time. I'll never arrive. I know it. My systems are just going to run out.

I wanted to be dead by now. Too many goddamn push-ups. Why did I make my body so strong? All that swimming. A goddamn waste. When it comes time to drown you can't do it, you keep going until the cold has eaten you molecule by molecule.

I'll never survive this.

I'd cut my wrists with my fingernails if I could find the strength. I can't keep my eyes open. There are only these few mo-ments after *linala* when I can sit still like a lizard and it's before the radiator fluid and between the coughing. There's room for going through the door. Once a day, maybe, a short trip.

If I'm sane still, this is what's doing it.

I'm walking in the tall grass with my family. The grass is way over my head and my father is in front of me, pushing aside the grass. We have rubber boots on, the black kind with orange and red soles. It feels like the first warm day of spring. I can smell the world thawing. There are buds on the trees but still a bit of snow on the ground in cold pockets out of the sun. I'm wearing a thick woollen sweater, knitted by my grandmother and sent in the mail from across the country. Dad has a big one on; he strides like a woodsman. Graham and Mom are behind us. I think of my soft brown peaked cap as my Confederate hat but it isn't quite that style. It feels new, thrilling, to be walking in woods, but it's old, too, elemental. I don't know why we're walking. Just to do it. To walk.

Still like a lizard, wounded, waiting for death. The air sliding in without touching any flesh. Eyes closed, blinking is too painful. Here is the door. Here is escape.

Walking in Britannia with Patrick and Maryse. Fall this time. The beach is chewed up with footprints from other, warmer week-ends. No one here now. I'm wearing my father's old woollen sweater. It weighs about eight kilos, feels good on my shoulders and arms. No wind can penetrate it. Maryse in her bright blue Gore-tex, in her tights and running shoes. The jacket goes down below her bum but I know what it feels like — to rub my hand around and underneath so that she stops what she's doing and her smile becomes a little distant. I don't do it here but only think what it's like. Patrick, too big for the stroller but too small to walk far, clutches the stroller and calls out when he sees a bird. The river looks low. It's been a dry season and the marshes are brown, depressed. Maryse is trying to go for a run but Patrick won't let her.

"Mommy! Don't go!" He shakes the stroller, crying.

"Just take off," I say to Maryse. "He'll be all right."

"Oh, honey, I'm only going for a short run!" she pleads, bending down, pulling a tissue out of her sleeve to wipe his face.

His hands go out, she picks him up, the crying intensifies.

"Just leave him with me!" I say. "He'll be all right as soon as you're gone. I'll distract him."

"Oh, fuck, I *hate* this!"

"Fuck!" Patrick says. "Fuck!"

"Oh, I'm sorry, don't say that! I meant fork!"

"Fuck!" Patrick says.

"Just leave him. I'll take him."

"I only wish he'd give me, like, half an inch of breathing room!" she says.

"You have to let him go to do that."

Uncurling his mitted fingers from Maryse's sleeves.

"Mommy!"

"It's okay, sport. It's all right. Maryse — just go!"

She turns and runs. A beautiful stride, light, fast, athletic. Her thick black hair streams back, unruly, free, those funny cords of grey looking like racing stripes. She can't keep up that pace. Won't. Starts to slow after a couple of hundred metres. But doesn't turn to look. Freedom, freedom.

"Buddy!" Patrick says, pointing from his spot in my arms. Not at Maryse, but at the seagulls circling the marshlands. There's a blue heron, too, still, so thin and dirty I almost miss it. They're dying this year — I heard it on the radio. No one seems to know why. I don't know if this is one of the sick ones. It's just standing like a stick in the cold wind, alone and out of place.

Patrick's wispy blond hair curls out from under his woollen hat and his eyes in this light burn dark brown. He sneezes suddenly and snot shoots down his lips and chin. I dig through my pockets knowing that I haven't a tissue. Patrick laughs as suddenly as he might have cried, his eyes full of fun.

Shaking with every cough, like I'm blistered from the inside.

"Kill me, please," I whisper to Josef.

"Eed! Ged stronger!" He spoons the *linala*.

I don't want it. It's reverse poison, keeping me alive. I'm clutched together, bones in a bag, eyes too sore to open.

29

"When they find me, you people are toast."

"Toasd? You wan toasd?"

Coughing coughing coughing coughing coughing.

"Pariahs. Fucking . . . international . . . pariahs. When they see
. . . what you've done . . ."

"You eed, ged strong. Lig Rambo!"

Hanging on, hanging, then coughing coughing coughing
coughing.

"Let me write . . . to my wife. For when they find me."

"Ride wife?"

"A letter. Get me a pen and paper. Please."

"Eed! Ged strong!"

"If I eat . . ." coughing coughing coughing. Sand in my windpipe, mud in my lungs.

"Eed!"

Fingers won't clasp. Eyes gone, too. Can't hold the paper steady.
Shaking, shaking. I make an M, long and wild, like something
Patrick would write.

Drop the pen. Josef picks it up for me but it won't go back in
my hand.

"Just kill me," I whisper, then coughing coughing coughing
coughing coughing. I mean to say, "Bury me. Don't let them find
me. Make an announcement but hide my body." But the words
can't come out.

This is how I die. Trying to write Maryse.

"Time to get up." Still dark. But a different dark. A gentler dark. It feels so wonderful to be here. My father's voice, his big hand on my shoulder, a gentle nudge but enough to wake me. Then he wakes Graham.

Breakfast is cereal, hot bacon, fried eggs, toast and orange juice, freshly squeezed, the pulp lining the glass. Graham is still almost asleep, his eyelids fluttering as some dream fights to hang on. We both wear white turtlenecks from Christmas and corduroy pants and sweaters that our Nana knitted, Graham's brown, mine blue. Dad sits at the table with his coffee quietly reading *The Manchester Guardian Weekly*, which comes in a plastic wrap and has paper so thin you're afraid you might tear it if you turn the page. He's reading about Vietnam — I can tell because of how his eyes narrow and his face gets a little red. The Americans are getting pushed out of Saigon. We watched it on the news last night at dinner.

"So much bloody crap," he says, snapping the page over so that it sounds like it's ripped but it isn't.

Some minutes later he says, "Can you imagine — sending your sons over to die in a steaming jungle, bombing the place into prehistory, and then pulling out with your tail between your legs? Can you imagine?"

Mom comes down now, pulling the strings of her robe as she walks into the kitchen, slightly off-balance, her hair rumpled on one side and her eyes looking in an unfocused way at the clock.

"Ron, what are you doing with the boys?"

"We're going to play hockey," he says, still mad about Vietnam. Then he looks at her. "You could sleep some more."

"Where are you going to play hockey?"

"At the rink."

She nods uncertainly, standing now with her hands in the pockets of her robe.

"Did you get some — "

"Everything is made, we're almost finished," he says, gently lay-ing down the paper and standing, walking over to her. "Let me walk you back to bed." He hugs her in the middle of the kitchen, his hands so big on her back, and she turns her face so that it presses, eyes closed, against his chest. Instead of going back up they just stand there rocking.

"Isn't it going to be hard in the dark?" she asks.

"It's going to be light soon. Bill" — he raises his voice but doesn't turn to me — "could you get the skates and sticks together? There's a puck — "

I know already where the puck is, on the shelf by the *National Geographics* in the basement. We have a complete collection since 1962, the spines yellow and black across shelf after shelf. Dad hates it when we cut out the pictures.

I get the puck and the skates and sticks. When I start back up the stairs all of the sticks point in the same direction, but after two steps one of them splays and then gets stuck in the railing, only I keep climbing and nearly pole myself backwards. Just before I lose my balance I catch myself and pull the stick back out, but then one of the skates falls and bounces down the stairs. It's Graham's — he should have tied them together.

It's just this moment, vibrant suddenly as a flash of sunlight. This moment on the stairs, small again, in a different life, heading up to play hockey. But I'm not going to make it up these stairs. It stops here. That's all there is.

"We don't need to waste a bullet," one of them says. It's in Kuantij but I understand it completely. Everything is clear as only a dream can be now. A dream or death.

"He deserves a bullet," Josef says. He's the one who has kept me going this long. "Look what he has been through. He deserves a bullet."

It's Josef who puts me in the chair by the wall, who wipes my face with the warm cloth like he's my mother, who secures my head with a pillow so I won't fall over. He's gentle in everything he does, uses only the lightest touch. I can't take touch now. Everything feels blistered.

"Josef — hurry, damn it!" says the other one. "We don't have time for this shit!" In Kuantij the hurry is much faster, the shit far uglier — a ravine full of shit, a quagmire of shit.

"If we just leave him, he'll die in a day," Josef says then.

"I thought you wanted to give him a bullet."

"He's a fighter. Maybe they will find him and he'll live."

He says it so slowly, as if he doesn't care that the IS is outside on the street, closing in. I see them from somewhere above my body, legions of them arriving, surrounding the block, bristling with weapons. Josef and his friend are dead men, too.

"He doesn't live," the other man says. He points his assault rifle at my chest.

This is all too lucid. I can't know what they're saying. I can't see them this clearly. The IS on the floor above, scattering furniture, bursting through closet doors. I can't know like this. It's another dream.

They're coming down the stairs.

"Kill me!" I say. "Shoot, damn you! Now!"

He doesn't shoot. I don't want to survive this. He turns his rifle and fires into the men coming down the stairs.

This is how clear it is: blood spurts from across the room onto my face and I can taste its saltiness. Flesh explodes and cordite sears my nostrils and the noise of automatic fire smashes inside my head like the bullets themselves. This is how I die.

It's an odd thing being dead. Utterly still and quiet. Dark and cold and alone. Not in a grave but a tomb. I can see nothing but there's still a sense of space. Earth isn't pressing down on me.

Bones to chalk. Flesh settling to soil. Blood resting now, puddling as in a swamp.

Coughing coughing coughing coughing coughing.

"Josef! Josef!" I call out, but my voice in death is feeble.

We're playing execution. Tony and his little brother Bob, and James Meade, whose father is in the RCMP, and Brenda from behind the vacant lot, who isn't entirely a girl since she plays hockey better than some of us. And my brother Graham is here and Mario from across the street, who has blond curly hair and skin white and pudgy as a Greek statue.

I'm stunned to see them after so long. James Meade has the machine gun, a hockey stick broken in the shaft, not the blade, so it's too short but it could be used for a goalie stick. The tape is worn off the bottom of the blade from road hockey. It's strange to think we'd play road hockey in summer, but we're all sweaty and flushed so maybe that's what we've been playing.

James says, "Okay, Mario!" and then shoots him right on the lawn. Mario takes the first bullet in the shoulder and twists, jolted into the air, then is hit again so both hands fly back and he lands on his side, bounces on the grass, then moans and rolls away from his attacker. James stops shooting but Mario continues to get hit, the bullets making his body buck and sway in an almost sexual frenzy. Finally he's still, face down, legs splayed, grass stains all over his clothing.

"Tony!" James shouts and turns to shoot him down on the driveway. Tony screams in pain and surprise and heads toward the grass before the bullets take him down. His death is much like Mario's but he twists more, and he clutches himself as if trying to keep his guts in. There's an odd mixture of fear and pleasure in this surrender — he finds it hard to keep from laughing, even as his guts are oozing out of him, and then when he's supposed to be still he looks around from time to time at the others.

"Brenda!" James turns his wrath on her. She withstands a blast without flinching, advances despite the hail of bullets. She has long black hair and wide shoulders and wears a baggy black sweatshirt because of her breasts. Everyone can tell she likes James by the way she looks at him. He's tall and thin and has wavy brown hair and skin as fine as a girl's and can catch a football like a frog pulling in flies.

"I'm shooting you!" James yells, waving his machine gun, but Brenda simply advances, her eyes looking dangerous. When she's just a few feet away and by all rights should only be fragments of flesh, James suddenly stops firing and cries, "Abandon stations! Abandon stations!" then turns to run. Brenda lurches for him, gets him by the waist, but he twists out of her grasp and then takes off down the road. Brenda starts running, too, and then we all howl and chase across lawns and over the curb after him.

This is a new game. We don't know what it is — it's just happening, which is the excitement of it. Brenda is a good runner but James is fast, his arms and legs working like oiled scissor blades. He opens up a twenty-yard lead, then ducks into McCloskey's backyard and across the Stephensons' deck. It's a daring thing to do. McCloskey is a grey-haired cactus of a man who hates us even playing on the road, and no one has ever gone into his yard before. But now we all charge across it screaming. And the Stephensons don't have children, but we thump across their deck as if it's ours, then keep on running, through the hedge and on.

Just running and running for the fun of it, for being able to, with air so fresh in our lungs it hurts and legs going faster faster, and there's no way to do this silently, we all have to yell and keep on yelling.

"Shhh!" Christine says. She sits up suddenly and looks around.

"It's nothing," I say. "Just kids."

"Oh, shit."

I try to turn her head back toward mine but she must listen now. I can hear two or three of them on the swings, somewhere down below. What are they doing out this late?

We're in a small fort in a play structure at the elementary school. It reminds me of being in a snow tunnel at night when it's cold outside but warm where you are, your jacket and the snow walls insulating you. It's spring now and cool, but Christine and I are both in leather jackets, pants and boots. It's all fabric against fabric except for her astonishingly tender lips, thin and warm and passionate. She has long blond hair, very straight, and her skin is too soft and her eyes don't close in kissing. I don't know how long we've been here — maybe half an hour.

"Hey, Ted, I think there's somebody up there!" one of the kids yells.

"What?"

"I heard somebody!"

The squeaking of the swings stops. There's a whiff of cigarette smoke.

"You go up."

"Why me? You go up!"

"Come on, go! Chicken?"

"Fuck off!"

A tense moment, waiting for them to come up the ladder, but they don't, they just go away instead. Christine is listening, listening, but finally I get her attention and we're kissing again. I move my hand along her jeans until it rests between her legs and she stops, clamps her thighs tight so my hand is wedged in harder. She starts to breathe deeper. She moves around to take more of my hand between her legs, and when I start to rub she makes small moaning noises. She's so tiny, thin and small, but her hair is long, long, and in sunlight her eyes are blue sky with just a wisp of clouds.

She climbs on top of me and pulls my knee up between her legs and rocks so hard my head goes bonk bonk bonk against the pillar of the fort, but her eyes are closed now and she's gone wild. "Uhnn UHNNN uhnn!" she moans, rubbing against me, and I shift my head, which she doesn't notice, to make the thuds less painful. She also doesn't hear the voices down below — "Shhh! Shhh!" the kids are saying to one another, "Shhh!"

"Uhnn UHHNN uhnn!" she goes, harder and faster, pushing against me, until she suddenly stops in mid-push, arching, mouth and eyes open — "AHHHHHNN!"

The damn bursts below. "AHHHHHNNN!" say three boys' voices at once, and then the laughing erupts and they pound on the sides of the fort. "AHHHHHHNNN! AHHHNNNN! AHHHNNNN!"

"HEY! FUCK OFF!" I yell, trying to stand, but Christine is on top of me still, and when I move her head thumps against the roof of the fort.

"Oh, shit!" she says.

"I'm sorry!"

"AHHHHHHNNN! AHHHNNNN! AHHHNNNN!" They yell it all the way down Clear Avenue, running like dogs. I watch them go, and when I turn back Christine is sitting in the corner with her legs drawn up, knees pulled against her chest.

"I'm sorry," I say, and sit back down beside her. I try to put my arm around her but somehow the space has become too small even for that. "Are you all right?"

"I need a cigarette."

She stays still a moment, deciding, then reaches to the corner where her purse is and fiddles a moment in the darkness, then pulls out a package of cigarettes and a lighter. She smokes hungrily, eyes down, turning the lighter over and over with her left hand while holding the cigarette in her right.

It's the first time I've seen her smoke. I had no idea.

It only takes a couple of minutes. We don't say anything. The smoke fills the little fort like we're burning up.

"I've got to get home," she says finally, butting out and rising in one practiced movement. She's so small she can almost stand up in the fort. When she walks away her step is light but rushed, as if she can't wait to put distance between herself and all that has happened.

"Josef!" I don't know if it's a dream. I'm trying to open my eyes but everything stays dark even when I think they're open. But dreams are tricky that way, too, because sometimes you can *dream* your eyes are open even when they're still shut.

There's no coughing, so it's a dream. In life I cough most of the time now. My throat and lungs feel as if they're hanging in strips inside my skeleton. And I don't feel that now. Everything feels all right. So it's a dream. The projected scenes going past me one by one — all dreams. This is not life.

Or it's death. It's all the scenes falling out. Spinning, spinning. Everything coming off now. Winding down. Coming up for a different kind of air.

The air is clear in the mountain camp, I can feel it washing over my skin like water. There are breakfast fires and women cooking at them, and children wrestling and running with sticks, and dogs barking after them, and mud puddles from the rain last night. I step out into the light and am dazzled, it feels almost like sunshine although it's overcast. But it's light, direct light! I turn around looking, looking. Tents, huddled back beneath huge-leafed tropical trees as if they're hiding. Everything dripping, sagging after the rains, except for the weapons, which lean against one another in a perfect circle, dry and gleaming, the wood dark brown and polished, the metal oily black. It's like the most brilliant photograph I've ever seen.

I move toward the weapons. It's marvellous having no pain, having my body again. The ground feels so far below me. I'm almost there when Josef suddenly sees me. I don't know how he sees me — I just feel him from behind and then he's between me and the weapons, standing with his feet planted, his hands on his hips. He carefully looks me in the eye, as if he's holding me on a line.

"You didn't make it from the room," he says. Again it's Kuantij but I understand every syllable.

"Josef. I'm better now. Thank you."

"You didn't make it from the room," Josef says again. "I was the only one who escaped."

"But that was a dream."

"You are the dream."

I head for the weapons but every step takes me further away. Draining, draining like a dream.

"This is not your place," Josef says from far away. It's the saddest thing, to lose the camp. To be back in darkness, back in the room. Feel the hood around my head.

Coughing coughing coughing coughing coughing coughing.

Silently now, stealing out of bed. The light is still on, leaking under the bottom of the door, so my parents are still up. I ooze out from between the sheets like a python in pajamas, silent death.

Graham's breathing is heavy, the fool — he's gone to sleep with death stalking him just one bed away!

Onto the carpet now. My eyes adjust. It isn't really dark. I can see the two desks and the two dressers and the outline of the curtains and Graham's form on his bed. Sleeping innocently. I creep along the floor, smooth as a snake, slowly, slowly. Death comes when you least expect it. Not even a rattle. He's snoring, the fool! I pause beside the humidifier, ease my way past it. Reach the foot of his bed.

Gliding, gliding. He hears nothing. He's in his own little world. His hand has fallen out from under the covers, hangs down halfway to the floor. I pause, look at it. Study my prey.

I keep my head low so he can't see me. Tickle, tickle. Gently. His hand flicks for a moment, then settles back where it was. I tickle again, a little harder.

He pulls his hand up and rolls over, nearly oblivious.

The python starts to climb onto his bed. Slowly, smoothly, so that his prey has no idea. No idea at all until it's too late.

"Death!" I hold his face, and he jerks awake, says, "AH!" in that movie way he has, believing it all, his eyes wide and panicked. He pushes up against me, but he's so small he can never get me off.

"BILLY! BILLY!" he screams, kicking now and crying, and my parents burst into the room with supernatural quickness.

"What in God's name are you doing?" Dad rips me off Graham and shakes me in the air by the back of my pajamas.

"Damn you!" Mom says.

"I was only fooling!" Graham is crying, of course, the way he always does.

"He just got to sleep! He's been coughing for two days!" Mom says. Dad throws me back into my bed. I fly through the air, then bounce off the bed, the wall, then the bed again.

"Ron, careful!" Dad stalks out of the room, too angry even to speak.

Graham is bawling, bawling, bawling.

"I'm sorry! I'm sorry!" I say, crying now myself. "I was only fooling! It was only a trick!"

"Billy always sneaks up!" Graham says, then he's coughing again, deep and horrible.

"It was just a joke!" I say feebly.

"I'm so angry with you, Billy, I just want you to shut up, all right? Don't you *ever* do that again, do you hear me? And certainly not when Graham's sick! Do you hear me?"

What? I thought I was supposed to shut up, and now I'm supposed to answer?

"I don't know what's wrong with you sometimes," she says, holding Graham.

Then when I close my eyes I have to listen to the coughing, coughing, coughing.

"My brother was in an accident," I say. I'm balancing on the arm of a sofa, half-sitting, half-standing, and the room is crowded. I have to be careful not to spill my beer. The loud music from the next room floods into this one but no one is dancing, everyone's yelling into the next person's ear.

"I'm sorry to hear that. Is he okay?" the girl says. I don't know who she is, except she has lovely hazel eyes and an intelligent tilt to her head. She might be a first year — she has that fresh look.

"I have to phone back," I say. "My mom wasn't too clear."

"Is he in the hospital?"

"In Edmonton."

She waits for more details. She has her legs drawn up, holds her beer bottle while clutching her knees. Faded blue jeans and a T-shirt from the university, and blondish curls verging on brown.

"Was it a car accident?" she asks finally.

"No, he fell. He was doing construction." As I say it I think of Graham in midair, turning over, his hard hat coming off, the boots that Dad bought for him weighing him down, steel shanks and all. It's an odd feeling, remembering the call that came as I was going out the door. Mom so short on details. She was heading to the airport, would call in the morning when she knew more. Nothing you can do. Just wanted to tell you.

Waiting, wondering. Going to the party anyway. With Graham falling, turning, his hard hat coming off and boots weighing him down. Not wanting him to hit the ground. Three-storey building. He was on the top. He was the only one who fell.

Laughter and loud music and smoke and beer, maybe a hundred people jammed into the student house, the doors left open to let out the heat. Winter outside, short sleeves in here. Other-worldly. Graham still somehow in midair. Thinking — he bounces well, Graham. He's a little guy but he's tough. Always has been. But not knowing. Then thinking — three storeys, that's too much, even for Graham. His boots pulling him down. But maybe he fell in snow. Maybe there was a soft, eight-foot drift waiting for him. It's Edmonton, they get a lot of snow, don't they?

Then this girl, surrounded on the sofa but all alone in a way. She reminds me of Christine. I don't know why — she has a different look, but is quiet like Christine, self-contained. Approaching her and thinking — my brother is falling off a three-storey building and I'm talking to this girl.

"Are you from Edmonton?" she asks.

"No."

I should ask her her name. What's she studying? What year? Where's she from? Does she live on campus? Can I phone her? I think of all these things to say, but I half-sit and half-stand beside her and watch Graham spinning in the air. He might be dead and I don't know it, won't know it until morning.

"I hope he's all right," she says. Maybe it's the way I look, or maybe it's the way I don't look. Everything is so strangely normal. I'm attracted to this girl. My brother is in a hospital in Edmonton.

"Thank you." When I'm outside with my coat and hat on against the winter I think how odd it is to be walking with Graham still in midair, twisting, not down yet.

On my knees. No clothes. This bone rack of a body. The pain of my shoulders and arms. Not thinking of anything. I couldn't answer any question now. What's my name? I couldn't say. Everything focused on this moment. Getting past it.

They all have cigarettes and I'm not supposed to raise my head. When I do I get burned. But I don't know which direction. They're all around me and I'm on my knees like a dog and mustn't raise my head. It's hard when you don't know if the burn will come on your back or buttocks or calf or the back of your hand. I'm so slow I can't see it half the time and then there's the surprise and I start to raise my head and get burned again. They're laughing, I don't know how many there are. The skinny one, a tall one with one finger missing, another man in heavy boots. Not Josef. Josef hardly ever comes when they're beating me.

Oh, shit! Why can't I keep my head down? They love it when I make a mistake. "C-I-A! C-I-A!" they yell. Sometimes Boot Man lands one in my ribs or stomach. I hurt everywhere anyway. But no fucking limit. Just worse and worse. I just stay still, panting like a dog. Still as wood. It's how they want me. I'll do it all the way they want. They'll stop then.

"C-I-A! C-I-A!" Aren't they afraid of getting caught? There must be people outside who can hear them. They're so loud and drunk. Fucking animals. They want me to be an animal too before they kill me. That's fine. I'll stay here still as a dog while they put out their cigarettes on my flesh.

But it's hard to stay still so long. I haven't any muscles left. Just holding myself up is too hard. They're yelling, they want me to make a mistake. It's what they want. I have to do what they want. I have to.

It doesn't matter, I think, when I'm on my stomach. Legs forced apart then they're pulling me up again, on my hands and knees, it doesn't matter. The burning on my backside. A different kind now. It doesn't matter. Their hard breath hot skin grunting pressing slamming fucking it doesn't matter doesn't matter doesn't matter —

Kill me. Kill me. *Kill me*, says the little part of my brain still dealing with this shit.

My eyes open and I see the room now not in darkness but in dull light, the remnants of the full tropical sun outside sneaking past the heavy window blinds. No hood for some reason. I'm immobile in a corner, more or less just piled here like kindling. Weak. Sharp pain in most of my body, so I'm awake, this is real. It won't last long. I don't remember when I last ate. Emaciated. Dying. Old already, certainly. Why have they left me? I don't know. Why isn't real any more. Why doesn't matter. I am and soon I won't be. That's all.

Old and shaking, my heart racing even though nothing is happening, I'm just here alone. Alone. But I'm never alone. I can't be alone. They've fixed me now. Ground my face into the floor. Don't think about it. I won't I can't I won't but still there it is, their breath and laughter and the fucking cigarettes and me naked face down spread. Close my eyes and there it is. Open them and everything is still and yet there it is anyway. Heart pounding, breath ragged, eyes here here here fists clenching unclenching clenching. Ha! Fists! What the fuck are they for?

Fists.

I want to castrate them. I want to carve out their livers, boil their feet, napalm them. Napalm their children. Infect them with deadly diseases. Ugly diseases. Flesh-eating bacteria. Viruses that chew out their organs slowly and can't be stopped. Microbes to turn their brains to bone. To make their blood run shit and their shit run blood. Cook their flesh slowly from the inside.

I just want them to stop stop stop, get out of my head. Take their fucking cocks elsewhere. Next time. Fists. Next time I swear.

God god god God god help me next time.

It's been a horrible flight. The air seems to be running out, my nose and throat burn with the aridity and the effort, over the sixteen hours, to get enough oxygen. The blower over my head has been on full for most of the flight but the air tastes and feels as if it's coming directly from the smoking section at the other end of the plane. All those Asian businessmen considering their stock options.

Maryse is sitting rock-still beside me, her eyes closed and lips drawn in a pose of enormous concentration. She has a migraine and every vibration of the plane shoots through her. Her skin is pale, almost grey, and clammy, and she's trying not to throw up. She has the bag in her hand and has already bolted to the bathroom twice. Patrick is asleep beside her, next to the window, big for four, thin and pale like his mother. Riding it out calmly. Where does he get that from? When did that start? It's hard to know when you only have one, but a lot of the other boys I've seen his age couldn't sit unoccupied for a minute and a half to save their lives.

They have to run *now* move spin walk around fiddle with something climb up fall down run some more turn on the TV forget about the TV race their cars bang their cars spill their juice go into the other room come back climb the curtains run away *now!*

I'm going to get sick from this flight, I can feel it in my throat. I'm going to get sick but Maryse will be worse with her migraine. She says I have no idea about pain. She's right. I have no idea. I don't want to have any idea. I just want to get this flight over with.

I look at the briefing notes on my lap with mild interest.

SANTA IRENE

Pop: 21,662,000
Capital: Santa Irene
Religions: Catholic 68%, Protestant 22%, Muslim 9%, other 1%.
Government: President General Linga Minitzh, Federation Party; elected 1978; state of emergency decl. 1981.
Economy: Tourism, textiles, banking, lumber (teak). Foreign remittances from ex-pat workers made up 38% of foreign currency earnings in 1993.
Recent History: Santa Irene was founded as a republic by current president General Linga Minitzh after a short but violent coup in 1973. His promise to hold elections was kept in 1978. Minitzh and his right-wing Federation Party won only 26% of the popular vote but a split among the opposition parties, most notably the leftist Democratic Coalition and the peasant party, Kartouf, left Minitzh with a slim majority. The government was dogged by charges of corruption and abuse of power that came to a head in 1980 when both the Democratic Coalition and the Kartouf were

banned. Many of the leaders were jailed while others, according to human rights groups, simply "disappeared." The Kartouf proved surprisingly resilient and launched an insurgency in January 1981, characterized by bombings of public buildings and assassinations of government and business leaders. A car-bombing in March 1981, which killed the ministers of finance and tourism, several leading investors and one suspected drug lord, led to the announcement of a formal state of emergency that has persisted to the present. However, military and political analysts agree for the most part that the Kartouf insurgency has been exaggerated for political reasons: Minitzh has not held an election since his slim victory in 1978, and the National Crisis Act (NCA) allows the government to censor all news coverage heavily and to limit opposition activities.

I flip over to another document, a blurry photocopy of an article from a newspaper called *Islander*.

THIS STATE OF AFFAIRS:
Why nothing works on Santa Irene
by Kojo

I've been trying to get a telephone line installed in my office for eight months now. I paid the fee — 86,000 loros — to Island Tel in April, standing in line for nearly four hours for the privilege. At least their office is air-conditioned. In fact, it is gleaming, the whole place done over in polished marble, with columns and expansive ceilings that would have done the Roman Empire proud. The line snaked down several corridors and nearly out the front door — people made a special effort to bunch up just inside rather than stay out on the street.

The last clerk, who finally took my money, gave me a thin slip of paper that had so many stamps on it that it was unreadable. The first four clerks had extracted enough personal information from me to fill two or three volumes of a biography. I bribed every one of them, of course, leaving 5,000-loros notes in the open bottom drawer of their desks. Most of the other notes in the drawers were brown ones, too, but I did see a purple in there, and even a gold 100,000-loros note. (Of course, if I were fortunate enough to receive bribes at Island Tel, I, too, would leave large-denomination notes prominently in my open drawer.)

Then the waiting began. It's hard to be a journalist in the modern day without a telephone. My new phone would be bugged by the IS, but at least I would be able to call the government press office to receive my latest story, or even — imagine! — install a fax so that the proper information, already correctly written up, could arrive at my desk in time for the afternoon edition. No more trips across town in impossible traffic to wait at the Ministry of Information for my text! I had my slip of paper. Where was my phone line?

I got an appointment in June for the workers to come. We already had one line in the office. It was secured by a senior staff member whose name cannot be mentioned here and who dines often with the President and his friends. That phone is inside an air-conditioned office where the door is almost always closed and the blinds drawn. This senior member is so experienced that his copy just appears, miraculously; most of the time he does not even have to come to work. (He has a telephone at home, too, I believe, and a fax machine.) At any rate, the Island Tel crew would not have to string a new line from the street — they would just have to install another switch and hook into the existing connection.

August came and no line. I went to Island Tel again, but this time the line-up stretched all the way onto the street, so I gave up. I tried phoning from one of the new American hotels downtown, but, of course, anyone *with* a phone knows that the phone company can never be reached. I went back in September, waited over three hours, and was finally told by a clerk (after I had bribed her) that my line *had already been installed!*

"But why don't I know about it?"

Another clerk told me that my application had expired. "Application?" I said. "I thought I had *bought* a phone line!"

"No, sir. You must see the Regional Director once your application has been approved."

"But where do I go for that?"

"I approve the applications."

"But mine has expired!"

"Perhaps it could be reinstated."

And it could. All it took was a gold note in her bottom drawer. I was taken directly to the Regional Director.

"Your application looks irregular," he said.

"It's a little crumpled," I said. "I've been carrying it around since April."

He cleared his throat and said "Irregular" again. His office, I have to tell you, was the size of a ballroom, and he had seven secretaries, any one of whom might have been mistaken for Miss Universe.

"How could we make it regular?" I asked him.

He studied it quietly.

"Perhaps I should go to the bank," I said.

My phone was installed the next month.

Now that I don't have to work so hard, I've been considering why Santa Irene doesn't work. Many writers have blamed the colonial tradition — all those centuries of dealing with the Dutch, Spanish, British, Japanese, then Americans. Things don't work here because of *liir*, the island spirit that says "Yes master!" while stealing from his drawer, sugaring his gasoline, losing his mail. An act of patriotism, sitting in traffic that doesn't move! Things don't work around here because of our tradition to passively infuriate any invading power that wanted to shake us into the modern world and have goods arrive, water flow and garbage cleared from the streets.

The argument is enticing, and it's well within the Island character to keep on sticking it to the Americans even decades after independence. We would rather do this than start to benefit from having just one clean hospital and schools that could stay open more than two months consecutively. (I will write about the school strike next week. I'm sure it will not be resolved by then.) But there is something that the commentators leave out when they make this argument, true as it seems: the unspeakable fact of the drug money in which certain segments of the society are awash.

Is Island Tel able to coat their offices in marble because of people like me who, eventually exasperated, leave 100,000-loros notes in everybody's bottom drawer? Of course not. Even a room full of million-loros notes wouldn't begin to buy marble from Italy. It's the tide of drug money that needs to get laundered, and that therefore washes through all sorts of government and quasi-government offices and even supposedly independent businesses like the one run by a friend of a contact. His restaurant downtown almost never serves a meal but makes a million US dollars a year. How does he do it? Take-out orders?

It's the drug money, of course. Being Santa Irene, we don't actually grow or produce any drugs ourselves. (We're obstructionists, after all. Think of how we ruined the rubber industry after the British left.) No, we just make it known that our police, customs and other government officials, if properly compensated, are not going to be so efficient as to actually open someone's baggage, or check the veracity of a foreign traveller's papers, or insist that banks disclose earnings and pay taxes. Why are there so many Colombians staying in fancy hotels in downtown Santa Irene these days? Have they come for the fine air?

Enough said. Or perhaps too much.

A hand-written note at the bottom of the page adds, "The author disappeared three days after publication, the editor a week after that."

I put down the papers. Patrick opens his eyes slowly, waking up from a deep dream and not knowing where he is but not being panicked either. Everything is new at his age anyway — why not wake up on the other side of the planet?

Not long afterwards Santa Irene comes into view. Patrick slides up the window shade and even Maryse looks out at the ocean and the blue sky. The window is a bit dirty, but the dark green of the island still looks dramatic after so much water, the mountains stretching out of view, the white sand beaches ringing most of the coastline. And there, unmistakably, is the capital, a brown cancer where the harbour pokes in on the edge of the otherwise beautiful island.

"Oh, God, is that where we're going to live?" Maryse closes her eyes and presses her temples.

Crying, sobbing most of the time. Nothing to do. Long stretches when they don't come back — when I don't want them to come back — but there's the fear and terror of the waiting. When they strap me in again. Don't want to think about it but sometimes can't help myself. Burning, crackling, searing from inside, like everything ripped open. Different every time, but the same.

Sobbing. About everything. What they've taken. What they've done to me. If only I hadn't. If only if only if only . . .

One different move. Why did we come here? Why didn't I get Beijing? Why wasn't Peter with me? This would've never happened with Peter. Never. He would've seen it coming. Shit shit shit shit shit!

Sobbing and sobbing. Thinking of that time in Edmonton, standing by Graham's bed. All the bandages, those two weeks waiting to see if his back would respond. "You just take one rotten step," he said. "You'd take it back if you could. But you can't."

Sobbing. Till I'm so dry I feel leathery from the inside, a beached fish. Get a grip, I think. But no. Reeling. Graham got better. He did. But how can I walk away from this?

Sobbing and sobbing and stuck in this time like a fly in glue.

"It's okay, it's okay, it's going to stop hurting in a while." My mother's fingers are warm, running back through my hair and squeezing behind my ear where it hurts.

It's dark, but there's a light on behind her in the hall. She has on her robe and her hair is long and loose, not tied back like during the day.

I give the glass of water back to her, feel the bitterness of the medicine still in the back of my throat. I hate swallowing it. It almost always sticks somewhere and burns.

"Am I going to go to school tomorrow?"

"We'll see in the morning."

Graham is sleeping in the other bed. He stirs, gets up, looks around and says, "Watermelons," then goes back to sleep. Mom starts to laugh and I can't help it, I start to laugh, too.

"What's he dreaming about watermelons for?" I ask, laughing, which makes my ear hurt even more, but I can't help it.

"Who knows? Sleep," she says, smiling, tucking me back in. Just that feeling of being tight makes it hard to stay awake, even with an earache.

"Watermelons," I say instead of goodnight.

They have Patrick. His voice rings out — "Daddy, where are you?" — and wherever I was evaporates. I'm in the hood, heart pounding.

"Patrick? Is that you?"

"Daddy," comes his voice again, clear as an angel's, and I know I can't give up, I have to survive this, no matter what.

"Patrick! Where are you?" I scream it again and again, each time my throat ripping a little more. Then I stop, wait for a sound, anything.

It's hot. Stifling. Must be day. They might have him in another room. He didn't sound close. Is he all right? Have they been putting him through the same shit? No. Impossible. It would've killed him by now.

Maybe they've just picked him up. Maybe they're going to start. The panic hits again and I jerk my hands and the rest of my body as if I might be able to wrench myself free. And the pain explodes everywhere at once, so that I nearly black out from trying to move. God! I'm a wreck. A complete wreck. They have my Patrick and I can't even struggle to help him. *"Patrick!"* I scream, and then there's noise. They don't usually hear from me.

Cigarettes. Heavy footsteps. I'm listening, listening for the tiny jolts of his feet slapping the ground the way they do when he's tired. Have they gagged him? Drugged him? How did they get him? What do they want?

"Patrick!" I yell again, just to know quickly if he's there. Nothing, then a sudden slap across the face. It seems muted somehow inside the hood, not meant seriously.

Patrick would be crying. If they had him. I'd be able to hear his breathing and they couldn't stop him from crying out if he saw me.

Saw who? I'd just be a broken man in a hood. Half-dead.

"Who you now Patredge?" Josef asks. His voice is ragged, as if he hasn't slept in a long time.

"Have you got him?" I ask. "If you've got him I swear I'll return from the grave to persecute you for the rest of your days."

"Who you grave?" Josef asks. There are others in the room, I can smell their sweat and smoke, feel their breathing.

"I heard my son's voice," I say, trying to hang on. This could make me crazy, I think. If they have him. If they mean to make him suffer even a fraction of what they've done to me.

"No voyze," Josef says.

"I heard it. Clear as anything. If you harm him I'll drive your souls to hell."

"You mebbe dream."

"No dream. I heard his voice."

"E-B," he says.

"What?"

"Little boy E-B."

"What does that mean? What are you saying? Do you have him? If you've laid a finger on him — "

"E-B," he says again.

"What the fuck does E-B mean? Damn you!"

But he just repeats himself until I'm so angry I feel I could burst my ropes and shackles. But I'm a broken-backed doll, bristling with pins.

"Baby E-B," Josef says.

"What? Who?"

"E-B. E-B only! No here!"

Finally I realize that he's saying Patrick was on the television in the other room. I heard his voice on the news.

"Asging, where-you? Where-you?" Josef says, and I can feel his smile, as if it would be funny for such a little boy to be trying to find his father. Then somehow I feel certain that by mentioning Patrick I've put the idea into their heads to kidnap him too. I don't know how I know this, but it seems obvious, unavoidable. They're going after Patrick. There's nothing I can do. It's my fault. If only I hadn't said anything!

Tears flood from me. Anguish for where I am and what I've let them do to me. Spineless, wretched. I should have clawed them, kicked, screamed, lashed out so they knew they'd have to kill me or be killed. Go with some of myself left anyway. So Maryse and Patrick would fly home. No waiting around for the Kartouf to come after them, too.

And now I *have* to stay alive. Not just alive. Alert, whole, not a wreck. I can't be returned to them worm-eaten but still breathing. Patrick needs me. He needs a whole father. Not a shell. Not a disaster.

"Food!" I say quickly, before Josef and the cigarettes depart. "Hungry, food, please! *Linala*, anything! Please!"

It hurts so much. I mean to try my best but it hurts so much. The clear jelly in my throat and the light cutting through the back of my eyes and trying not to want the needle. The needle makes it bearable but takes away alert. I need alert. If there's a chance I want to take it. I'm flexing now, all day, exercise. Fingers and toes, calf muscles, shoulders, what's left of them. Working up and down the muscles of my body, one set after another. Flex and relax. Flex and relax. So if I get a chance I'll be able to move, won't be a lump of sawdust.

Trying to remember. That's the hard part, when you're isolated, packed away, no light sound touch only pain. Want the needle so bad. So bad. Flex and relax. Stomach. Painful because of the coughing, coughing, coughing, the lack of food and water. Everything running through me. Surprised I'm not dead. Wanted to be. Wanted it. Wanted.

But have to stay alert. Stay who I am. Don't know how I'll get over this but there'll be a way. For Patrick. Must make it through. And not as human garbage. Want to walk out.

Walk out. Flex and relax, flex and relax. Don't think I can stand on my own. Have to get over that. Work on it. Work and work. Have to help myself. If there's a chance.

Jesus, just once more for the needle. Want it so bad. Needle takes me out and away. But not to who I am. Somewhere else. Strange.

Not the needle. Flex and relax. Stay alert. You never know. It's possible. Maybe. Maybe it is.

"It stinks here, Mommy," Patrick says.

"Yes, you'll find that," Peter says. "It takes a while to get used to." He's tall and angular and surprisingly untanned. He's wearing an open-collared, short-sleeved shirt, which is a relief. I'm baking in my suit, but I wanted to make a good impression coming off the plane.

Peter steers us slowly out of the airport parking lot. Maryse is in the back with Patrick. She looks pale and otherworldly and is focused deep inside, still dealing with her migraine.

"Is this a bad day?" I ask Peter. "As we flew in the air was brown all around the city."

"It's the diesel fumes," he says. "All of the *tritos* use diesel — it just comes out thick and black, unfortunately. And we're not even close to getting an environmental protection law."

"Sorry — all of the what?"

"The *tritos*. The bus taxis. There's one!" he says, and there it is indeed, a chromed up, rainbow-coloured, punched-down bus with people crammed inside and out, sitting on the roof and hanging off the railings. "That's how most people get around. They're kind of fun but dangerous, too. There aren't any set routes, the driver just zips around looking for fares while his partner collects the money. And it's very competitive, so you'll get these guys cutting in on one another, racing down the street, trying to get to that old lady with the chickens first. There's a really horrific accident about once a week. A driver who's been up all night plunges into a ravine with thirty passengers, and a mob will beat him to death as he crawls out of the wreckage."

We barely make it out of the airport grounds when the traffic stops. The beautiful highway is completely jammed with little sedans, like the one we're in, and *tritos* piled with people. The air conditioning in the car is blasting but the air is still hot and smelly. Peter puts on some classical music.

"So I guess it was a long flight?" he says, gazing in the mirror at Maryse.

"The air was bad on board, too," I say.

"Look, Mommy, machine guns!" Patrick says.

I look to where Patrick is pointing. Even Maryse opens her eyes. Soldiers up ahead at some kind of checkpoint with black automatics on their shoulders and larger guns mounted on tripods. No wonder the traffic moves so slowly.

"With the diplomatic plates they'll wave us through," Peter says. "But we have to get there first. You have to be philosophical about it."

"About what?"

"Sitting in traffic in Santa Irene." He says it with the Spanish pronunciation — *Ee-ray-nay* — which sounds so beautiful I make a mental note to use it myself from now on.

We're waved through the checkpoint just as Peter promised, but at the next checkpoint we're stopped and a soldier goes through our papers closely. He looks about fifteen, nearly drowned in his uniform. And yet the mounted machine gun trained on our car is very real, its large belt of ammunition gleaming in the sun. After we get going again Peter says, "When I first arrived I used to hear them firing off their weapons sometimes at night. For no reason, really, just to celebrate. But it's been much quieter recently."

"You've been here for — ?"

"Three years," Peter says. "Right from start-up. Normally we wouldn't have an embassy in a place like this, we'd cover it from Manila or Bangkok, but this was part of the whole South Asia trade initiative. And there's a lot of money flowing through this country."

"Drug money?"

"Not all of it," he says. "A lot of running shoes are made here now. There's a big break for the multinationals. Brand name shoes are dirt cheap. And they're starting into computer parts, but that's a tough business. Labour is still very cheap all over the region."

The edges of the city now, what seems to be a near-random collection of low, stained buildings, with fields of rock and waste, and then the brilliant green of huge-leafed trees, and more buildings with cracked-tile roofs and broken steps, chickens pecking in dirt yards and children sitting in the shade, watching. Patrick presses against the window, quiet, taking everything in.

"What do you think?" I ask him. He doesn't respond, just looks, looks, looks.

"What are you holding me for?"

I ask the question when the *linala* has stopped burning in my throat and the whiteness of the light isn't so overwhelming. It's just before Josef will put the hood back on me.

"Whad you say?"

"What are you holding me for? What are you hoping to get?"

"Resd Boo-reej. No tog."

"You have to tell me — why are you holding me? Maybe I can help you."

"Resd Boo-reej."

Flex and relax. I can hold my head up better. The exercise is working. My fingers not so swollen anymore. I can handle the spoon.

"Is it prisoners? Do you want some people released? Do you want money, arms? UN protection?"

"Togging too mudge. You resd Boo-reej."

"Maybe I can help. Get me a telephone. I can talk to people at my embassy. Maybe we can grant you asylum. In Canada. Do you want to go to Canada?"

As I ask the question he spoons out more *linala* which I eat greedily. I have to get better. I have to get stronger. If I want out.

"It's cold in Canada, but only in the winter. In the summer it's hot like here. Where I'm from — Ottawa. Extremes of hot and cold. But you get used to it. The life is good. Have you ever seen snow? Do you know what I'm talking about? Snow and ice?"

"Boo-reej — quied!"

"Talk to me, Josef. This can't be going well for you. You're as much a prisoner here as I am. You meant this to be over before now, didn't you? Tell me what you want. I can help. I hate the IS, too. I know what they do. You've done it all to me. You've done everything. Everything you can. You didn't mean this to last so long, I know. It was supposed to be over quickly. Let me help."

"Boo-reej — tog and tog!"

I do talk and talk. Say anything that comes into my head, trying to keep my wits. While I'm talking the hood is off and I can see where the door is, the draped-over windows. The way Josef looks when he isn't completely in control.

"Is it prisoners? Are the IS holding some Kartouf? You want them released?"

"Now ded," he says. "No las long I-S."

"The IS kills them?"

"No las long."

"Is it money, then? You want money for arms? Medicine for your kids?"

"Tog too mudge."

"Let me help you," I say, spooning in the *linala*. I say it and I keep saying it until the hood goes on me again.

Back to my hole. I call it that because I can't see where they put me. Cramped though, tiny. Uncomfortable.

Flex and relax. Focus and remember. Who I was. Who I am. Who I have to be.

The staircase to Maryse's apartment has thirty steps or more. I've been coming here half a year but I'm still not sure of the door until I'm almost upon it. It's dull red and decaying and doesn't close completely. You walk along Dalhousie with the traffic and the slush and, at night, the hookers shivering in stockings and down vests, smoking and searching. I watch and watch, then there's the door, and I go through it as if entering a cave, the stairs leading up into darkness. A vagrant is sleeping there, huddled out of the wind, wrapped in old clothes and the smell of personal rot, with no easy way to get by. Jason, one of Maryse's roommates, clears vagrants away fairly regularly, but he must be out tonight. I step over a cold-blistered hand, stop a moment despite myself to look at the bearded wreck of a face. He appears to be in his seventies, might be fifty, might be younger.

I push his hand under the fabric but kick a little snow on it inadvertently, then clumsily brush it off. He groans in his sleep, turning to press against the wall in an elemental movement, as if pressing against a mother's breast. I climb the rest of the stairs, further into darkness. Two doors at the top. To the left — unknown, Maryse has never seen the tenants. To the right — a strange refuge.

"Oh, you're here. I was wondering," she says when she opens the door. She's in blue jeans and a red silk turtleneck that she found at the Salvation Army. Barefoot because it's so warm living over Hangzhou Heaven and Take-out Restaurant. Fine toes, robust, nicely spread. Like they've walked most of their life in sand.

"It got crazy at the office just at five-thirty," I say, stepping in. I want to look at her again before we kiss. I have a strange feeling still of not being sure of her features. That black profusion of hair with the cords of grey, strange because her face looks so young, late thirties by her hair, early twenties by her skin and the eyes staring straight into mine. I'm a bare quarter-inch taller.

"Your office always gets crazy at five-thirty," she says. I unzip my jacket and she pulls it off me and dumps it behind her on the stairs. "You should leave at five."

I laugh. "Yes. Imagine that. Leaving at quitting time."

"Or get there later in the morning."

"They'd love me for that."

"You don't have to get there before eight o'clock."

"Except when there's a conference."

I have my boots off now and she pulls me up the stairs, collecting my coat on the way.

The apartment is dark as always, but through the gloom as I climb the stairs I glimpse the bicycle parts hanging on the wall in the living room and the pyramid of dead TV sets — the art of Lorne Popup.

"Sorry, your name is Lorne Popup? Pleased to meet you—I'm Maryse's friend, Bill Burridge. I've never seen bicycle parts on the wall before. Except in a bike shop, I guess. What made you choose the name Popup?"

"My parents chose it. It's my name!" Snakes of blond hair twisting in front of his eyes, the back of his head shaved nearly bald.

No music tonight. Sometimes Lorne's band, Sintax, practices in the spare room on the main floor. Jason plays with him — a different instrument every time. Nothing traditional. They were playing toasters one time, rattling tire irons in tin cans another. I pass a huge brown sludgy canvas on the stairs, something new. It looks like shit waiting to drip and lump on the steps. But it has no smell — it's lacquered to neutral perfection.

"He's into texture now," Maryse says when she sees me inspecting it. "It's not staying. He sold it to someone from Montreal who's going to come with a truck. They're hanging it in a bank or something."

Maryse's room is the first on the right at the top of the stairs, across the hall from Lucy, who lives in a perpetual state of comical instability. She keeps falling in lust with customers at the restaurant, always seems to be running down the hall to the bathroom with a sheet around her body and her hand in her hair saying, "Shit! Shit! I'm late, shit! Jesus!" Tonight her door is closed. She's probably working.

And on Maryse's door is a comic book explosion of electrical tape squiggles left by a previous tenant. These things I notice or think just in the moment it takes to go through the door.

"Are you hungry? You must be starving," she says, pulling me onto the futon by the wall. There's a small computer on the huge oak desk that was her father's, and the poster by the window is Monet's water garden painted when his eyes were clouding.

"Are you hungry?" she asks again, rolling on top of me, pinning me between her knees, pulling at my tie and collar.

"Famished."

"That's too bad," she says, tugging my shirt open, kissing down my chest. "I've already eaten."

The feeling is magnetic and electric, candles and stars and old radiator pipes that warm without burning, no matter how close you get. In a rush to get naked I jam the zipper on my trousers and break a shoelace. She laughs and pushes me under the covers as I fight with socks and underpants and a watch strap that won't release. She's black hair and ivory skin, soft shoulders and strong hands, molten in the mouth. "I've been waiting for you," she whispers.

It's over too fast. She lies huddled and quiet, her back to me, the thick blankets pulled over her and her knees tucked up. I spoon against her back, which she endures for a moment, then makes a little turning movement that gives her more space. "It's so hot," she says a little sharply, yet she pulls the blankets over her even more. Then — "I'm sorry" — she turns back to me, draping her leg over mine. She has such long bones — her hands a little bigger than mine, her long neck. I lightly kiss her breast, so pure white. I remember the poor man on the stairs.

Maryse says, "Before you came I was doing very well. I found this place on my own, I was working well, I slept nights. I didn't sit around looking at the bloody clock to see when you might get here."

"Oh, listen, I should have called. I'm sorry. But you said — "

"Everything was solid," she says. "Now I can't — "

She stops and looks away.

"Can't what?"

"It doesn't matter. Are you hungry? You said you were famished."

She gets up suddenly and pulls her clothes back on, stands by the dresser to brush out her hair. I wrap myself in the blankets, watch her in the soft light. Could easily fall asleep. She goes down the hallway to the bathroom. I turn over and close my eyes, feel no hunger at all for anything but rest.

Le petit mort. How still and sad. One time Maryse and I were talking about how long you stay dead. Vast time. The life of the earth, of the universe. Our own little strut. "Maybe life is the orgasm," she said.

I fall asleep for what feels like a minute but wake up cold, my left shoulder especially sore and numb. It's then that I notice a hole about the size of a child's fist in the wall by the corner of the futon. Through it I can see part of a streetlight on Dalhousie Street. The cold wind pours in.

"I'm sorry, I couldn't wait for you, I got hungry again," Maryse says as she walks through the door, chewing on the remnants of something.

"You've got a hole in your wall," I say. "In the corner. Do you see?"

She sits on the chair by the desk, still chewing.

"I want to see you," she says.

"My shoulder's frozen. It feels like cold meat."

She doesn't say anything, just looks at me in an intense way.

"What?"

"Nothing," she says, chewing and smiling.

"What?"

"I got a contract today," she says.

"That's not what you're smiling about."

"Public Relations. They want a poster and a pamphlet series. I did what you said. I asked for too much money."

"Terrific! Good for you!"

I start to get out of bed, gather my scattered clothes.

"Where are you going?" she says, wiping the crumbs from the corner of her mouth.

"I told you, I'm starving. And I have to pee."

"Well, that's too bad," she says.

In a half-moment that's like a lifetime I realize I'm not going to make it out of this woman's bed. Not tonight, not for the years and years it's going to take to know fully the way her gears shift and emotions swing, the slope of her thighs and the rich coffee of her laugh and the way she'll stay up half the night worrying about a re-mark until all at once she'll know exactly what to do, and how hidden in some soft corner will be the quiet breath of our children. It's a sudden certainty that somehow seems attached to her, a point of feeling that could never have come without her, and for a moment I'm overwhelmed with the weight of it.

"What?" she says, looking at me, pressing her warm fingers against the coldness of my shoulder.

I hate it when teeth fall out. They rattle loose and then get caught in the back of my throat, and I think of these bits of my body falling off like a riverbank falling away. I have eleven left. My tongue — my swollen, lumpy, aching, thirsty tongue — can't help but travel over the empty spaces. Taste of blood in most of the holes.

Cankers, something ripped on the roof of my mouth. I can't remember them putting the clip there but it feels like they must have. I black out most of the time before they're done Am so disappointed to find myself back here.

One long drink of water a day. I think that's what it is. Or else that's what a day is for me: the time between water. It only seems to make me feel worse. The pain in my stomach. Hunger — constant, gritty, greedy. If I could just resist the water when they bring it. Two or three times — two or three days — that would do it. It's so hot. Stifling. I'd just faint away. They hardly ever look in on me. I'd be gone before they'd realize it. The great escape.

I plan it over and over. The next time the water comes I'll refuse it — shake my head, just have a bit, spit that out when they've gone. It's so hot anyway, filthy, probably contaminated. Which will kill me faster, drinking or not drinking? I'm alive now and that's been too long.

I plan it, steel myself, make resolutions. But then the hours stretch on and, dizzy as I feel, I still want the water. Worse and worse. I haven't the will to give it up. It's so stupid. A spineless nobody like me should die for lack of will. But that's what's keeping me here. Not enough will to refuse the water when it comes. What could dehydration feel like compared to what I've already been through? It couldn't last long. I'd lose consciousness, a bonus already. They'd find me but too late.

I plan it, but it doesn't matter, when the water comes I open my cracked lips and the relief is nearly too much to bear, I cry almost every time. Giving back the salt I'm drinking. Sobbing, nearly choking, the hand holding the cup so strangely gentle. I want to refuse but I can't, I'm such a spineless fuck.

Nail in my spine at the base of my head. Can't flex, can't relax, can't escape. Constant pain. When I cough bombs explode inside and around. Tremors. Shaking and chills. No way to stay still. Nails everywhere. Try to flex. No flex. No escape. No way.

I wanted to hold on. Patrick, believe me. Maryse. I wanted.

With every breath thinking, die now, die now, death. Please come. Come now, please. End this. End it. Over. Now.

Like a train wreck in super slow motion. Caught on the tracks. No way to escape. Caught in slow frame after slow frame. No way to speed it up. No way through it.

I don't even smell the cigarettes. Just sudden light. Flinching from sharpness, jagged in my eyes and brain. So painful, more and more, takes everything over.

"What? Josef, what?"

"Vee day! Fill-um!"

"What's that? What?" I say, and they drag me into the bright room. Two of them, with Josef walking ahead. He's the one in charge of this. He's the one to persecute from the grave.

But there won't be a grave, only a slit body in the harbour. If there's any body left.

They dump me in a chair, push my shoulders back so that my head stays up.

"Still!" says Josef, but the coughing coughing coughing takes me over. Everything wounded.

"Still!"

When my eyes clear there's Josef pointing a video camera at me. It seems so incongruous, the tiny, perfect piece of Japanese machinery here in this basement, this medieval torture den.

"Tog! Boo-reej! Say — Boo-reej O-K!"

"Medicine," I say, trying to look into the camera. Lights suddenly very bright. Blinking my eyes. And the nail again in the base of my neck. Every movement painful. Breathing. Not breathing.

"Say Boo-reej O-K!"

"I need medicine," I say, but I know the words don't come out clearly. I don't want them to make this film. I don't want Maryse and Patrick to see me like this. Stick limbs and drool and rotting body.

"Say O-K. Boo-reej O-K!"

I lift my head, trying to see through the lens. Whoever's behind there. Whoever's going to see me like this.

"Burridge O-K," I say, as firmly and as loudly as I can.

The TV screen is fuzzy, as usual, but it's not going up and down. Last week it went up and down and Dad got angry with it, started pulling tubes out of the back. But this is just fuzzy, more grey than black and white. A double image, a ghost around the trunk of the car. There's something inside. The reporter's voice goes on and on. There's a body! Mom and Dad sit white and cold at the dinner table. They don't say anything when I drop my fork, full of twisted spaghetti, onto the floor. Crash! They don't say anything, don't look away from the screen.

"What is it?" I ask and they shush me, tell me to listen. I am listening. I can't understand it. It's the news. The news is bad. Somebody found a body in a trunk.

The picture changes to another man standing in front of a microphone. Two men, almost, as the shadow grows. "Damn this set!" Dad says, throwing down his napkin. When he gets up though the two men blend back into one. He stays one man for about a minute, then slowly starts to divide into two again. I start to giggle. I can't help myself. Dad gets up and the picture goes back to normal. Up and down, up and down, till I'm laughing my head off, I can't help it, it's so funny.

"*Quiet!*" Mom screams then, banging her open hand on the table so the plates and spoons jump. She's furious. She's going to have a baby. *"Listen!"* she hisses so I do, I try. The Prime Minister is on now. Pierre Elliot Trudeau. I know him. He can do a jack-knife off a diving board.

We listen all through dinner. Mom and Dad are grim, not eating. I try to understand, but I don't know what's going on. I ask again but Mom tells me again to be quiet, she'll explain later. The commercial comes on and Mom says, "You will not go outside without our permission, do you understand?"

"Why?"

"That man in the trunk. The one who was murdered. That was Pierre Laporte."

"Pierre Laporte." I say the name as if I know who he was.

"He was kidnapped by the FLQ," Dad says. "And now they've murdered him. They're still holding Cross."

"James Cross," I say. FLQ. It stands for something in French. I know that. "He's still kidnapped?"

"You are not to go outside without our permission," Mom says again.

There's more on the TV, much more, the whole evening is FLQ this, FLQ that. It's hard to get away from it. At night, when I close my eyes, right away the FLQ tries to get me. I can't see them. They don't have any faces. But Pierre Laporte's body was in the trunk. Why do they put it in a trunk? When are the police going to find Cross? FLQ. They're hiding in the shadows. Can't be caught, no matter how hard you try. First they got Cross, then Laporte, now Laporte's dead. Just like that. Body in a trunk. Cross is probably dead, too. He's probably in a different trunk only they haven't found it. I'm walking along somewhere, it's hard to know where, everything's so grey and blurry. But they're after me. The FLQ. They want me. I start to run but they keep up with me in the shadows. I can't see them. That's the problem. You can't see them. They're everywhere but they're nowhere. You can't catch them and you can't see them. The FLQ.

I turn and try to get away and turn again and run but there's no way, I wake up scared and crying. The FLQ. It's so dark now. The whole house is dark and cold. I creep out of bed. Could the FLQ run in and grab you out of your house? I bet they could. They're that wicked. Monsters. They killed Pierre Laporte and left him in a trunk.

I walk into Mom and Dad's room, quietly, quietly. The light's off but they're lying still with their eyes open. Mom knows immediately that I'm in the room. She doesn't say anything, just holds out her hand so I go to her side. I snuggle up against her and she rubs her hand up and down my arm. She's so big. She's going to have a baby. You just get bigger and bigger and then the baby comes out.

Everything's warm. I close my eyes but all I see is the letters painted on a brick wall: FLQ.

"Slow down," the nurse says.

"I'm sorry. I just got in from the airport. I'm sorry," I say, catching my breath. "My wife's name is Lorraine. Maryse Lorraine. She's in labour."

The nurse looks in her register. She's older, in her forties, her pink outfit stiff and almost garishly clean, as if made of some plastic, dirt-repellent substance. There's a pocket for pens, and her cuffs aren't just folded back, they seem bent into place, solid and geometric.

"C-223, on the left," she says. "She's resting."

"Resting?"

"It's a boy," she says. "A really beautiful boy."

"Oh, shit," I say, then catch her startled look. "I missed it, that's all."

"Visiting hours are over, but you can take a quick peek."

"Thank you."

I walk down the hallway with my suitcase and overcoat, my footsteps echoing the way they did at three airports in the last sixteen hours. I feel as if I'm in someone else's skin, taking someone else's steps. Stand on the Great Wall with your camera. Watch bicycles massing in Beijing. Drink green tea from mugs with lids and eat candies and exchange pleasantries with old men who nod and laugh and laugh and nod. Sit in a heated bus drumming up immigration stats on a notebook computer while peasants pull cabbage carts on the street. Hurtle home. Step down this evening hallway. C-223. Behind this door is a brand new person.

I turn the handle, walk in quietly. My eyes take a second to adjust to the muted light. I look at the first bed on the left: a plump woman reading a glossy magazine, her glasses large and rectangular, her blonde hair curled tightly. On the right is someone with grey hair, turned on her side, sleeping, her face obscured. Past her is an empty bed, and on the other side a dark-haired woman who is not Maryse — she's much older, with pasty white skin and a deflated body.

There's no one else. The nurse got the room wrong. I start to turn. But the dark-haired woman looks up to see who it is, catches my eye.

"You're here," she says in a flat tone that wedges in me. Her eyes are dull, drained of life.

"How are you?" I ask. She doesn't answer, just holds out her hand, and I walk to her.

"Oh, God, it was awful," she says.

"Are you all right?"

"I'm never having another baby."

"What happened?"

"I just . . . he wouldn't come out!" she says, and then the tears start and I hold her.

"I got on a plane as soon as I could."

"Oh, I needed you," she whispers.

"You'll be all right. You'll be all right."

She's sleeping in a moment, which makes me think she must be on some kind of medication. Was there tearing? Did they do a c-section? I don't know. Just that I wasn't there when I should have been.

I retreat quietly to the nursing station.

"Is it possible . . . I haven't seen my son yet."

"Oh, the lights are off in the infants' room," she says. "Tomorrow, eight o'clock. You should get some sleep."

"I'm kind of jet-lagged," I say. "I was in Beijing sixteen hours ago."

"Do you want something to help you sleep?"

"No, no. Thanks."

I walk to the elevators, then turn back.

"Um, was it a difficult birth? Was there an operation or — ?"

"Sorry?"

"My wife is wrung out."

"Well, that's childbirth," the nurse says, a little flippantly and with a secret smile. "It was pretty clean, actually, and a lot of first births are slow. She'll be a different woman in the morning."

"Thank you," I say, and then say it again, because there's nothing else I can think of.

They want me awake for the beatings. It's such an effort — I don't want to be awake. Just kill me. Let me go somewhere else. Slit my body, feed me to the sharks in the harbour. I know you know how to do it. I know that. Who said that? Somebody said that. I know for a fact . . .

Without the hood is the worst. No, every time is the worst. I shouldn't think of this. Keep it out of my mind. Mind away. Spirit elsewhere. Somewhere else . . .

But all I see is the tall one. The one with the gentle eyes. Like he's pleading with me. Burridge, we know you can speak Kuantij, we know who you are. Why do you make us carry out these acts? All this through his eyes, the reluctant way he dips his head. I'm sorry, he seems to be saying. This is so unnecessary.

Attaching the wires. Those fingers thick and dirty, like they've been rooting around greasy engines since boyhood. Making sure I'm looking. Doing it slowly, meticulously. Those sad eyes that seem to be talking. Are you sure we have to go through with this?

"I'm sorry! I'm sorry!" I say it over and over, in my head and out loud. I know I used to know Kuantij. I was in the CIA. It's true. It's all true! Yes, yes, yes! I'll tell you anything. Anything you want to hear. But I can't remember any of it! It's been exploded out of my brain! I've tried and tried and I know you want me to try again but there's nothing left, it's blasted away. I'm sorry. So sorry. Please. Please!

Those fingers pinching the rusty clips. Making sure the wires are attached properly. My arms and legs and head and hips tied down with rough ropes. But I can see his fingers, cut and dirty.

I don't want to think about this. It's over, it happened already. Already gone. There must be other things to think about. There must be. But my brain won't stop it, won't shift gears. Brains can think of different things. I remember that. From before. There was a before. If I could remember . . .

Using his nails to twist the ends in tight. Tough and sharp, like a pair of pliers. I've already been through this! It's in the past. Stop it! Stop it right now! Brain, I command you! Think of something different! You can do it. I know it's possible. *Please!*

His fingers moving so slowly, and all the time he's talking. He doesn't look as young as his voice. He looks as if he's walked in from a year in the jungle. Lean and hard and old and still. His voice too young. Speaking as if he knows I understand. I should, I know. I'll tell you anything. But I can't remember. Honestly! This thing you're doing now — it's not going to help. You know that, don't you? This won't make me remember better. It's going to fry me from the inside. You know it will!

Shit!

I shake my head, breathe hard, kick out trying to get away. It's just in my head! That's the stupid thing — it's all happened before and I lived through it and there's no need to have to go through it again. Do you hear me? Stop it! *Stop!*

But I can't make his hand stop. It's reaching across my body now. I can see everything. Those rusty clips. Clamping onto my nipples, my scrotum. Staying there. His voice never stopping. I try to twist but the ropes hold me tight.

His voice always the same, saying the same things over and over in Kuantij. I should know it. I know I should! But I'm not who I used to be. I'm *different*. It's not my fault. You don't have to reach for the box.

The fucking box. *No!* I'll tell you, it's not me. Do you hear? Put the box back. All right, I have an explanation. Don't hook up the wires. You don't need to. There's no —

Shit!

I jerk hard, writhe, my teeth clatter. This isn't even happening. Burridge! Get a grip! You went through it! You survived it! Don't think! *Don't!*

Air ripping from me screeching rigid flailing like I'm skinless running from a burning building but not moving, can't move, just have to let the flames broil the air slamming in and out don't damn it don't damn it don't!

No! I howl because I already lived through it and *this is past*, this is different time now, I don't have to relive it, don't have to keep shaking burning slobbering freaking out, it's gone!

I hit my head *huhn huhn huhn!* against the stone wall until blood seeps into my eyes and the sharpness of this new pain takes his hand off the switch in my brain.

Second day of work. I don't wear a tie but an open-necked island batik shirt of brown and gold, long and untucked in the local businessman's style. It feels odd, as if work isn't really work, but the illusion disappears at the post, where thirty-eight interviews have been lined up with people waiting for immigration papers. Peter is apologetic.

"Normally we give new staff a few days to get a handle on things," he says, standing in his office with files under his arm, talking as if we have only twenty seconds to spare. "But Marianne left for school in Houston and Robin was burned out. So it's just you and me."

"How long was Robin here?" I ask, blocking the door, buying time.

"He and Marianne came together, when was it, two years ago?"

"And they've split up?"

"It was ugly. We were lucky there wasn't a homicide. I'll fill you in later. Can you and the family come for dinner sometime?" He's pressing to get out of the office.

"Yes, fine. Wonderful."

"Use 204 for the interviews. Lila should be in to translate. They're very bad on documents and we've been more lax than we should be, so insist — passport, birth certificate, national registration. If they have a degree you want to see the original. Not a photocopy. We've had so many PhDs arriving in recent weeks it's unreal."

I don't even know where room 204 is, but Peter is halfway down the hall.

"The files are in Dinta's office," he calls. "If you have any questions, I'm just upstairs." And there he goes up the stairs, leaving me alone. I head down the hall to Dinta's office. She's a tiny woman, perhaps in her fifties, with large, questioning eyes, her long hair tied in a tight bun.

"How do you like it so far?" she asks, her voice slow and musical, as if the whole day spreads luxuriously ahead of us.

"It seems a bit rushed," I say.

"Don't worry about that. It's only the Canadians who are rushed. Nobody else expects you to be on time."

"Well, I suppose that's reassuring."

She opens a large mahogany file cabinet and a burst of birds erupts out of it and flies out the open window. Unperturbed, she takes out a group of thin files.

"What were the birds doing in there?" I ask.

"Oh, don't mind them." She hands me the files. "These are the people who are supposed to come today."

"Supposed to?"

"Sometimes they trade with their cousins, or they sell their interview slots to someone across the street. And when we issue the actual visas, we have to be sure they aren't taken up by someone else altogether."

"Ah."

"Peter has informed you though about all this."

"No, actually, he hasn't."

"At any rate," she says, "Lila will know."

In room 204 Lila is already talking to a young man with nervous eyes who's wearing a blue polyester suit and drumming the table with work-scarred fingers. Lila is a stunning beauty in a white blouse and flowered skirt, her thick hair hanging free to her shoulders. I introduce myself and she stands and shakes my hand with a good, firm, western-educated grip.

"This is Mr. Dojomondio," she says in an English accent, and he bows his head severely, as if ready to kiss my feet.

"Right, fine," I say, sitting down, flipping through the files to find the right one.

"I'm opening a new file for Mr. Dojomondio," Lila says, so I stop flipping.

"Wasn't he on the list for this morning?" I ask.

"He was on the list, but he did not have a file."

"I see." I have no idea whether or not that's significant.

She speaks to him at length in Kuantij. I make a careful notation — MR. DOJOMONDIO — on my notepad and wait for the translation. But Mr. Dojomondio replies at length in Kuantij, then Lila explains something to him, pointing at a form, and then Mr. Dojomondio speaks again.

"Excuse me," I say, after this has gone on for some minutes. "What's happening here?"

"I've just been asking Mr. Dojomondio why he wants to immigrate to Canada. And then we were going over the points system, which he doesn't understand."

"Ah."

She motions to the form again and goes on again in Kuantij, then Mr. Dojomondio stands up, his head still bowed, and thrusts his hand at me.

"Very please!" he says, bowing, smiling, backing out the door with the empty form.

"How did we leave it?" I ask Lila, before the next one comes in.

"He has another appointment next month," she says, then reaches down to her briefcase to pull out another file.

"Who's that?" I ask.

"Mr. Wijitanga," she says and goes to the door to call him in. He's an older man with little hair, a round belly and silver front teeth. He too smiles and bows and thrusts his hand at me.

"I think I should ask the questions on this one," I say as we all sit down at the table. I pull Lila's file toward me.

"Now, Mr. Wijitanga, you're a teacher, is that correct?"

Lila translates, but takes two or three minutes. Mr. Wijitanga nods his head finally at the end of it.

"What did you say to him?"

"Just what you asked," Lila says.

"You seemed to say a lot more than that." I try to be authoritative but friendly at the same time.

"It is customary to engage in pleasantries at the beginning," she says. "We do not just plunge into business."

"Ah," I say. We pause while everyone waits for me to say something.

"Are there more pleasantries to engage in?" I ask Lila finally. She gives me what I've heard referred to as an "island smile" — a devastating flash of light from a truly beautiful woman — and she says, "No, we are fine."

"Good, then, Mr. Wijitanga," I say again. "You're a teacher by profession, is that right?"

Lila translates, but again goes on at some length. Finally Mr. Wijitanga nods again.

"What — were there more pleasantries?" I ask her.

"Before speaking of professions, yes," she says. "I was praising teachers and the work they do."

"Could you tell Mr. Wijitanga that we have a surfeit of teachers in Canada, and that that profession, honoured as it is, has been closed to our immigration lists for many years."

Lila does this in three words, as far as I can tell. Then Mr. Wijitanga explains something at considerable length, pointing to imaginary things on the table, then rubbing his neck, his chest, and his forehead swiftly with his right hand.

"What's he talking about?"

"Mr. Wijitanga is a teacher of *ganaliba*, of traditional medicine," she says. "He has cured many cancer patients and can remove gallstones and throat abrasions without surgery, just through manipulation."

"Gallstones and throat abrasions?"

"Yes," Lila says, and Mr. Wijitanga nods modestly.

"Does he have a diploma or certificate? Did he undergo professional training? Does he teach at an institute or hospital? Is this a recognized form of medicine?"

Lila enters a long, apparently reluctant debate with Mr. Wijitanga. After one exchange he turns away from her completely and starts addressing me, the words jabbing like knife strokes. Lila interrupts him and he turns to address her again, the argument building and building until abruptly it stops. Mr. Wijitanga turns in his seat and glowers out the window. It has just begun to rain, the drumming on the leaves and rooftops quite loud.

"*Ganaliba* is well recognized on the island," Lila says to me. "At least in the mountain villages, everyone believes in it. There is one institute in the capital which is studying *ganaliba* systematically. But Mr. Wijitanga is not affiliated with them."

"Who is he affiliated with?"

"He said his teacher was Kili Wontoyamo."

"Ah." At the name Mr. Wijitanga turns to me and nods solemnly, as if accepting congratulations on behalf of his teacher.

"Who's that?" I ask Lila finally.

"A famous *ganaliba* master from one of the villages."

"I see." I look at my watch. "Could you tell Mr. Wijitanga that his application would stand a much better chance if he could raise some interest in, uh, this type of medicine — "

"In *ganaliba*."

"In *ganaliba*, yes, if he could interest a Canadian teaching hospital or research institute in it. I'm sure we have appropriate lists. But he'll have to write the letters, get them translated, make the contacts. Because otherwise this is an unknown practice in

Canada. There might be NGOs or health groups that would be interested in sponsoring him . . ."

Lila makes her speech, and Mr. Wijitanga listens carefully, with more solemn nods. Finally, when she seems to be finished, he reaches into the small black case he has brought with him and pulls out several oversized bills. Lila shakes her head and motions *no* to him, but he reaches across and pushes the money at me anyway.

"I'm sorry, sir, I can't accept this sort of thing. Lila, could you explain to him — "

She tries, but he gets up quickly and turns away when I try to push the money back at him. He's almost at the door when I reach his pocket from behind and shove in what money I can, two of the bills falling out almost immediately.

"Mr. Wijitanga!" I say, but he doesn't turn around. I'm left waving several bills in the hallway, a roomful of Santa Irenian hopefuls watching me.

"We have a special basket," Lila says to me when I retreat to the interview room.

"What's that?"

"For the bribes we are unable to return. It's a charity basket. There is an orphanage where some Canadians in the past have adopted children."

"Ah," I say.

"You will get used to it," she says finally, flashing me an island smile again.

"Josef." I'm back at the jungle camp. It's nighttime now and someone is frying fish and vegetables over a fire and some children are singing, but I can't see them. He doesn't seem too disappointed to see me.

"Are those your children, Josef?"

"What do you want, Burridge?" he says. When he speaks it's pure Kuantij and yet I understand it all.

"Are any of those your children?"

"No." He's cutting a pineapple with a machete, slicing out the spines in a spiral motion.

"Josef, what's happening to me?"

"I told you — you are dead."

"I'm dead already?"

"I told you."

"But I'm not. I'm here."

He doesn't answer, just looks down at his fingers while he's cutting.

"Josef, I have a wife and child. What has happened to them?"

He cuts, cuts, cuts, the sticky juice sliding over his hands.

"I must know. Are they all right? Has the Kartouf harmed them? I must know!"

He gets up and walks a distance away. Two children run right by us, oblivious, and Josef kicks at a dog that sniffs up at his pineapple.

"Josef!"

He turns to me. "We are being hunted like animals," he says. "But that is not your concern now. You are finished with all of this."

"I'm not finished with it!"

"Then trade places with me!" he says, standing, holding out the drippy pineapple.

It's such an odd dream. I reach for the pineapple, but Josef gets further away until I'm watching from the edge of the camp, from a ridge away, from down in the valley, where the dinner fires are pinpricks of light, barely visible, like rumours of stars behind clouds.

"Now this one you have to look out for," Peter says, pointing with his spoon to a dish in the centre of the table — squarish lumps covered by bright red sauce. "It's a fruit called *tarwon*, but the sauce is very spicy. Quite a delicacy here, but Westerners usually have a hard time with it."

He's much more relaxed away from the office, charming and at ease. His house is splendid, very open, with high ceilings and polished floors and a swimming pool out back. I don't know why a single man gets a swimming pool when a family doesn't, but I suppose if you've been around long enough these perks fall your way. Patrick is perched on Dinta's lap, playing with his food, and Lila is sitting next to Peter, looking cool and gorgeous in a red batik outfit with a pattern of interlocking lizards running all over it. Somehow the way she's sitting makes me think she and Peter are together, though there's no real evidence. For no reason, too, I'm sure that Maryse has noticed and that we'll talk about it in the taxi back to our house tonight.

Maryse is wearing a new dress that she got at Wexfords, the shopping mall for rich people near the government section of town. She calls it her diplomatic dress, something she'd never have worn in her previous life. It's white cotton with blue stripes and buttons up the front, short-sleeved. She knows how well it fits and keeps glancing over at me and smiling innocently. She's talking with an Australian woman whose name I can't remember. I have to get the hang of introductions if I'm going to be a diplomat, get those names to stick instead of sliding away immediately. The Australian woman has bushy brown hair and happy, easy eyes, and has steered around all the meat dishes. Marlene, there, that's her name. Marlene the Australian vegetarian. Maryse has quietly been extracting the details of Marlene's life, snippets of which I catch from across the table. She had an unhappy romance and was one credit away from a nursing degree in Melbourne when she abandoned it to work with the village children in the mountains north of Santa Irene. She rides up in the morning on the regular bus, but it's slow because of the roadblocks, so she's hoping to be able to stay in the villages for longer periods. Her Kuantij is very good. She saw soldiers drag two boys off the bus the other day. They hadn't done anything wrong that she could see, they were just village boys.

"That's happening more often," Peter says, and the several conversations around the table become one. I try the squarish lumps in red sauce. My throat burns suddenly, and my face flushes so hot I burst into a sweat. "The government has become obsessed with the Kartouf," Peter says. "It's something to be aware of."

I quickly take a glass of water, the burning subsides for a second, then comes back as soon as I swallow, so I drink again, trying to be inconspicuous. But even breathing becomes hard, and tears run down my cheeks.

"Sorry, the what?" Maryse says.

"The Kartouf. It's a rebel movement based in the mountains. The government is fighting it by rounding up village boys. Actually, it's misleading to talk about the Kartouf as a single entity because there are so many factions now, they're very loosely knit. They had some backing from Iran, of all places, because the founder converted to Islam for about a year. But it's not a religious movement at all. Probably we should have some training on them. I'll see if I can get Bruce Wilson from the State Department to come over. Are you all right, Bill?"

"Fine," I croak, gulping more water, the sweat now pouring down my face and my mouth feeling blistered.

"You had the *tarwon*?" he asks.

"Yes." I try to show that I'm all right, but no other words make it out.

"Oh, honey!" Maryse says, standing up.

"The water actually makes it worse," Peter says, as I drink more. "Lila, could you ask Min for some yogurt?" Lila excuses herself and I have to close my eyes because without the water the pain is searing.

"What's the matter with Daddy?" Patrick asks.

"Maybe some ice?" Maryse suggests.

"No, the yogurt is best. Just hang on, Bill."

For several agonizing minutes the dinner party stops completely while I grip the tablecloth and focus my thoughts on the next moment, the next moment, getting to the next moment.

"I did the same thing once," what's-her-name says, the Australian vegetarian. "It hurt for a whole day. The islanders love it."

Finally the yogurt arrives. I spoon it in hopefully, feel the coolness of it creaming against my wounded throat and cheeks. I open my eyes and again try to say, "It's okay now, I'm fine," but the words come out unconvincingly between gasps.

"I'm sorry, I should never have served the *tarwon*," Peter says.

I spoon in more yogurt. Gradually my mouth cools down. Peter talks a bit more about the factions. Patrick spills his juice on Dinta's lap and she laughs in the most infectious way, almost dancing as she pushes away from the table, holding Patrick and wiping herself with a napkin at the same time. Maryse apologizes again and again but Dinta just keeps laughing. Children can do no wrong here, especially boys.

There are more dishes, but my taste buds have been traumatized. I call it a near-death experience, which gets everyone laughing, but the pain and the heat and the hammering of my heart were very real.

"They use chilis in their torture here," Peter says nonchalantly over coffee. "The IS. They're brutal. We'll be having dinner with some of them on Saturday."

"What's that?" Maryse asks.

"There's a reception on Saturday at the Pink Palace," Peter says. "It's black tie. They have them about every two weeks. Honestly, they just love protocol. Everyone who's anyone will be there. And the IS people — Intelligence Service — are the most charming of them all. Really. Most of them have spent time in Washington and

London. They've been trained by some of the best. And they love what they do."

"What do they do?" Maryse asks.

"They brutalize people, especially village boys, whom they suspect of sympathizing with the Kartouf. Even if they don't suspect it they'll sometimes brutalize them just to send a message to others. You won't read about it in the newspapers, but there's a body problem in the harbour. Or least there was. I think it's been sorted out by now."

"A body problem?" I ask.

"Yes. The IS were disposing of their bodies, the Kartouf boys, by weighing them down with cables and rocks and pitching them into the harbour. The cables only last a certain time, and then the bodies bloat up and float to the surface. A lot of them, I gather, are taken out to sea by the tides. But fairly often they washed up on shore. Their hands and feet would be bound and there'd be burn marks and welts all over the bodies."

"Burn marks?" Maryse asks.

"From the electroshocks," Peter says. "It didn't get reported, really, because it would have been damaging for the tourist industry. But some months ago the bodies stopped turning up on the beaches. Roger Davis from the CIA told me that the IS are now slitting the bodies open before sinking them, so they won't bloat."

Peter has been careful not to say any of this in front of Patrick, and when he and Dinta come back from playing in another room the conversation switches.

"Who was Saint Irene?" Maryse asks.

"A Christian martyr," Peter says, evidently pleased with the question. "In Macedonia. She was hauled up in front of the governor along with her sisters and some others for failing to eat food that had been offered in sacrifice to the gods. She resisted all sorts of pressures, and was finally thrown naked into a brothel for 'moral punishment.'"

"Oh, my God," Maryse says.

"But she emerged with her virtue intact — only to be hauled up again for hiding sacred texts. With her life on the line, and in front of the governor, she refused to implicate any of her friends. Finally she was burned at the stake along with her books."

"So this place is named after her?" Maryse asks.

"Yes, of course," Peter says, "although there is some debate. The first European here was a Spanish explorer named Enrico Vasquez. He and his crew went through purgatory to get here — they were down to about twelve men from the sixty they started with. They suffered storms, scurvy, they were even attacked by a sea-monster, Patrick." No rise from the boy, he's exhausted, we really should be going. "Anyway," Peter says quickly, realizing his storytelling time is running out, "most people believe they named the island Santa Irene in memory of her suffering and steadfastness. But Irene is also the Greek goddess of peace, and there's a minority school of thought that says they were so thankful for this refuge, this peace of paradise, that they just called it Irene, and the Santa was added later when the island became part of the trade routes and the missionaries arrived."

"Room for both, maybe," I say, standing up, getting ready to go.

"Purgatory and paradise. Yes!" Peter says, also rising. "Most diplomats come to that conclusion after about the first week."

Patrick's asleep in my arms as we wait on the verandah for the taxi. It's pouring rain, the night is slippery, obsidian. Peter's gardener manages to find us a taxi, Peter tells me to pay the driver 1500 loros, and then we pile in the back seat, soaked from just the moment's pause to open the door. The driver speeds us through the streets of Santa Irene as if we're in a James Bond car chase. The only working wiper is on the passenger side of the windshield so he has to lean over to see. But I stop thinking about it after a minute when I lose track of the streets. We're completely in his hands. I'm too tired even to worry.

"How's your mouth?" Maryse asks.

"It's okay. It's better."

"I was worried," she says, and kisses me for a long time, Patrick snuggling and snoring slightly on my lap, the driver speeding us to God knows where.

I was wrong. We don't talk about Lila and Peter. We don't even talk about Santa Irenian torture methods or the Pink Palace. We just kiss and kiss until suddenly we're stopped and home. I fumble over the money and try to ignore the driver's disappointment, staged or otherwise. Then we dash once more through the drenching rain, and even stripping Patrick, toweling him down, and pulling on his pajamas doesn't wake him. In our own bedroom we're much less gentle with our wet clothes, and I swear in the darkness that I can see steam rising from Maryse's body.

They must have got me some medicine. The chills and shaking have gone now, the nail is gone from the base of my neck. There's just the usual throbbing, pathetic pain. I try my routine again: flex and relax, flex and relax. The first time I only get halfway through — down to my bum muscles — before I'm exhausted. But it gets better. After I rest I try again and make it to my toes, then later twice through. Like riding a bicycle. The muscles remember.

Xiangyixiang. Think it over. *Laoda.* First child. *Huai le.* Spoiled. *Mei shenme.* It's nothing. *Zoagao.* Rotten cake.

Chinese phrases suddenly fall out, in perfect pitch, not in my voice but in Laoshi Wang's. All those hours in the language lab, utterly useless. *Chi gua fanlema?* Have you eaten yet? *Bu chi gua le.* No.

Starving. They're starving me. No way to survive that. Except I have to. Must. How can Patrick move past this if I can't?

I think of an article from some newspaper I read a long time ago. Everything seems like a long time ago. Someone else's life. That's why I have to remember. Not just remember. Hold onto the details. Life is in the details. Otherwise a waste. A huge waste. All of it rushing past.

The article was about how to live a very long life. Scientists had found a clue. Starve yourself. That was it. When the body thinks it's being starved it becomes extremely efficient. Every particle of nourishment is saved and used. It's good for the system.

Second thing: have your sexual organs removed. Eunuchs live longer. Is that right? How many ridiculous things have scientists discovered? A hundred and fifty years without food or sex. What kind of a life is that?

I have another mantra: bring the needle, bring the needle, pray to God, bring the needle. Where is God? God is in the needle. My fine thought for the day. Irene the Christian martyr had God to turn to, to think of, to bring her through the brothel with her integrity intact. Those were God's flames that took her, so she felt no pain. Peter told me. In another lifetime. There were other lifetimes. Many of them. Some things slip through from one to another. Mostly they don't.

A new theory: I really *am* in the CIA. But they planted a microchip in my head. The minute I was captured my whole past got wiped out and replaced by this fake one they've invented for me. That's why all these scenes keep spilling out. They seem new and old at the same time. It's all in the microchip that the CIA planted. There's a firewall. I can't access the other side. But I know there *is* another side.

Irene had God but I have the needle. Therefore the needle is God. And God *is* the needle. My smooth brain clicking over the logic. God takes me from this current shit-hole existence. The needle scrambles time in a kaleidoscope. The needle takes me away from this wreck of a body. Abandon ship! Alight somewhere else.

Otherwise I would have died.

Otherwise . . .

Shit! I hate this sort of thinking. How to die? Don't take the needle. Refuse God and death will come. Peace of the worms. That's it. It's so simple. Refuse the needle. Refuse water, *linala*. Drown in the bitterness until all the pain receptors have shut down. Without the receptors there is no pain. Pain does not exist. Cancel the devil.

To cancel the devil you must also cancel God. They feed off one another. No needle comes death comes peace no pain. No God?

I'd make that trade. Cancel God to cancel the devil. In my head I'd make that trade but the core inside me won't make it. Can't! Can't refuse water, *linala*, must have the needle if it comes. If it comes. Please God, bring the needle. Yourself in chemical form. Deliver me from evil if only for a short while. Whose voice is that? That voice of prayer? I'm not religious. *Yea, though I walk through the valley of the shadow of death.* I don't know who the fuck I am anymore but I know I'm not religious. *I know that.* So who is it at my core sending up these prayers, scrambling my will whenever the water arrives? Two, three days of being resolute and I could be free of this pointless pain. But for that weakness inside. Is that God? Screaming to protect himself? Torturing me even more than these fuckheads?

God at the root of this agony? A slimy egotistical selfish omnipotence who wants his glory at any price? What could it possibly matter that I survive an extra day? In the great fucking scheme of things? I'm talking to you, God — I've found you now and I am not overwhelmed. I'm fucking furious! You oily little desperate voice in the core of my weakness: *take the water have the needle more linala you can make it I know you I've known you all your days Bill keep going you know you can make it a little more just a little more you can do it I'm with you have some more stay alive.* Not just cheering but commanding. Life, life, at all costs, and why? To keep *you* alive. I'm more than willing to cancel you to cancel the devil. An even trade. Sweet human logical portion of my mind clicking over: you *are* the devil. Big enough for both parts. Cancel one and you cancel the other too. Peace of the worms. I'll take it. Not tomorrow — right now! You little shit.

The water comes and *linala* and I say to myself I will be strong, I will be strong but strong isn't good enough, strong takes you nowhere against God. The sweet release floods like any miracle in a Cecil B. De Mille spectacular, fills me with remorse and confusion, feeds the voice for next time, next time, next.

Next time I'll refuse, I say to myself when the scummy water has made it safely down my throat.

"Aren't you going to the dance, dear?" Mom asks. I'm listening to *The White Album* full blast through my headphones, but I know from her lips and the situation what she's saying.

"I decided not to," I say, closing my eyes and shaking my head to the music, hoping she'll go away. She pulls the headphones off.

"I thought you were going with Christine," she says.

"No." This house is so small and the stereo is right in the living room where there's no privacy.

"Did you have an argument?"

"*She* had an argument." I flip through a *Time* magazine, glancing at pictures of bombed-out Beirut buildings. I'd like to be a war correspondent. That would be good work. You wouldn't know from one minute to the next if you were going to continue to be alive.

"What was the argument about?"

"It was about, uh, you know."

"No, I don't."

"About, like, are we too young, and where is this going, and what do I want, and what does she want."

"What *do* you want?"

I put down the magazine. I want to listen to some really loud music.

"She thinks I'm serious but really I'm not serious and she isn't serious so if neither of us is serious then what's the point?"

Mom nods, sits on the sofa beside me where I haven't invited her.

I say, "I really want to work this out on my own."

"You do?"

"Yeah." I roll the magazine and slap it against my thigh a few times, trying to think of what it is I think.

"The thing is," I say, "I really believe that with love you're on your own. I mean, you have to work it out alone. There's nobody there to help you."

"There isn't?"

I slap the magazine, *whack whack whack.*

"No. You go into love alone." What I mean is, when you face the emotion and power of it you have to be yourself, which is to say alone, as an individual. You need the courage to face it alone.

"It's so strange having boys," she says finally. She looks at me whacking the magazine, so I stop. "My sisters and I would gab all night about things like this. We'd never do a thing without complete consultation. And here you and Graham are, towers of silence."

I reach over and switch off the stereo. Christine doesn't have any sister to consult. She's completely on her own.

"I think I *will* go to the dance," I say.

"You will?"

"Sure. Could I borrow the car?"

The exhaust is going on Mom's Pinto and the door freaks when you slam it because of the rust. It's less than a mile to school but it somehow feels right to drive. I've had my license now for a month. I'm wearing my old jeans and my brown leather jacket and my tennis shoes from last season. As soon as I start the car I think I should go back and change into better clothes, but then, I think, the lights will be off in the gym anyway.

I get cold on the drive over. It's a spring night but there's a wintry wind and the heater in the Pinto died in January. It only takes five minutes, but by the time I'm in the school parking lot I'm shivering. I should have worn a sweater and gloves. I park the car and jump out, and there by the shop entrance a group huddles, smoking and drinking. For a second I think I see Christine, but it's hard to tell in the dark. Kevin Toll, in a black jacket and tight pants, kicks out suddenly at somebody with his pointed boots, and the two of them feint and dodge one another, laughing and spilling beer, and the girls in the group turn to watch the display. I go around to the front entrance with my hands in my pockets. Mr. Lund, the vice-principal, stands near the door in the same beige suit and tie he wears every Friday. He looks as if he'd suddenly dry up and die if you took him out of the school, like that woman in *Lost Horizon* who left Shangri-la.

The marble-tiled floor of the school goes *thud thud thud* even though the gym is at the other end of the building. There — I wanted loud music. The halls look odd in this evening light, the lockers pale yellow and so many kids lounging around, which would never happen during the day, not with Lund on patrol. Now he's only a silent cop at a party.

There *is* a cop outside the gym. He's the size of our biggest football player and keeps a hand on the leather holster of his pistol as if he might need to use it, and he looks at all the girls as they pass by. More dresses and makeup than I've seen all year. This is such serious stuff for them. Maybe that's why Christine didn't want to come. Maybe that's why she started in with "Where are we going with this?" and "I don't know, Bill, I'm not sure." She's totally psyched by the different cliques of girls. She's smarter than most of them, though not at school, and so beautiful it makes me breathe funny just to see her.

I pay my two bucks and duck into the gloom of the gym, past the clumps of guys who look just like me, slouched in old jeans and running shoes with their hands in their pockets. I should have put on something nice. My father's right on that. You have to dress for the occasion. It never hurts to do it and usually makes a difference. I feel like any one of these losers.

A silver ball whirls in the middle of the gym ceiling throwing diamond clusters on everyone in the blackness. It's a slow dance, one of the chokiest songs I can think of, "You Are So Beautiful." I lean against the wall under the basketball hoop and hook my thumbs in my belt and watch. About a dozen couples clutched together, revolving slowly. In the far corner a DJ sits surrounded by big speakers and boxes of 45s. There's a light near the control panel and his head looms balding and huge, with headphones on, but he isn't bopping in time to this sap — he's listening to something else. It seems like the funniest thing I've tripped over all week and I'd love to point it out to somebody, but at the same time I don't really want to talk. I've just come here to be alone in a stupid, twisted way.

Someone lights a joint not too far away and the smell travels quickly. I'm waiting for Mr. Lund and the cop to storm in together, but nothing happens. The dopeheads are getting away with it, I think. And then I see Christine. She is here after all, standing in the shadows with the group that's smoking the pot. The cop is right there in the entrance looking the other way and they're toking and laughing and "You Are So Beautiful" is choking on and on. I take a couple of steps towards her. She's completely in denim and has put on too much makeup in order to fit in with the other tough girls, and they're all standing around Michael Ormond, a minor hood somehow still enrolled even though he hasn't seen a

classroom since November. He has long bad hair, his face is a bat-
tlefield, and he looks skinny and sick and likely to pull a knife on
you or puke or laugh in your face, you can't tell which.

I shouldn't go over but my feet don't listen to my brain. The
music changes to something disco and Christine starts moving to
it right where she's standing. She's stoned and her limbs are loose
and her eyes empty. She doesn't see me until I'm right next to her,
and when she does she says, "Oh God."

"Let me take you home," I say.

"Oh God," she says again.

"Burridge, fuck off!" Michael Ormond says. *Fuck off!* is an ex-
tension of everything he says, but this time he really means it. Out
of the corner of my eye I see the cop turn around and notice us.

"Come on, Christine." I reach for her hand, but gently. She
could rip her arm away but doesn't. "Come on," I say, tugging her
a little.

"Get your fucking hands off her, dickhead!" Ormond looks as if
he's made out of cardboard, but he has two friends right there just
waiting to punch me in the stomach and the cop is on the way
over anyway.

"Come on!" I say, stronger, and pull Christine, but this time she
does react, she yanks her arm in, and one of Ormond's goons
pushes me right into the middle of the dance floor. I fall and slide
on the waxed tiles into somebody's legs, knocking her over right
onto me.

"What the fuck are you doing?" some ninth-grader yells at me,
and as I'm trying to get untangled from his date the cop grabs the
collar of the guy who shoved me and everyone else scatters into the
darkness.

"Sorry! Sorry! *I'm sorry!*" I say, and the girl's dress hikes right up
to her bra for an instant as she struggles away from me. I help her
up and apologize four more times and lose sight of Christine. The
cop drags the guy out of the gym. People crowd around, gaping

and talking. I go outside. Around the corner, where the outdoor basketball courts are, Michael Ormond and four others are huddled together. I stand looking at Christine about thirty yards away, and she stands looking at me. The moment goes on and on. I think of kissing her and the weird things that she made happen with time and my body and how hungry she is for tenderness and the rage of her mother at three a.m. and how hopeless school is for her and the way I keep wanting to put the pieces back together.

We look and we look, and I don't want to be the one to lower my eyes first but neither does she. And Michael Ormond knows enough not to say anything. But I won't take another step and neither will she, and the night is cold, cold.

Finally it seems stupid and I turn to go. The Pinto freezes me all the way home and my mother has waited up, but I don't want to talk about it.

"How are you, Josef? Are you all right?" I ask him as I spoon in the *linala*, trying to sound casual. My heart is pounding with the thought of the food. I'm so hungry.

"Eed, Boo-reej."

"It's delicious. It's great. Josef, you're looking tired. Are you all right?"

He looks exhausted, hunted. We haven't moved for a long time, but this must be wearing him down.

I'm sitting better. The spoon now hardly shakes in my hand. I feel almost as if I could stand. Almost. Want to try it. Would give anything to try it. But can't with him here. He might decide that I'm strong enough again. For more.

Can't look too strong, I think, so I make the spoon tremble in my hand. Maybe I can fool him.

"Josef, how long have I been here? How long have you held me?"

"Eed, Boo-reej."

"Has it been a month? Do you know a month? Thirty days? Longer than that?"

"Eed!"

I am. I'm spooning it in. I can hardly get it down fast enough. It's so slimy and clear. I remember I used to think it was tasteless. But it seems strong to me now, almost sweet. Whatever's in it is helping me get better. I'm such a spineless shit for taking it, but whenever the moment comes I'll take anything, the needle, *linala*, scummy water. God wins, you see, every time. God and the devil both.

"A lifetime, it feels like," I say. "Don't you think?"

He just looks at me.

I'd like to ask him if this is simply another job for him. I can't remember reading that the Kartouf was kidnapping foreigners. I would've known about it. Peter would've told me. So this is new for him, I think. There must be international pressure.

"Why are you doing this?" I ask.

He looks at me.

"Tog less. Eed more!" he says.

"But why are you doing this?"

"Show vee-day," he says suddenly, pride all over his face. "Merica, wurld show vee-day."

I look at him, unsure, till I realize he's talking about the video. That pathetic clip.

"So now they know the Kartouf? America and the world?"

"Whole wurld Merica!" Josef says.

"Minister Alijo, I'd like you to meet my wife, Maryse. Maryse, this is the Minister for Preservation, Mr. Alijo."

"Mrs. Burridge, it is a pleasure," Alijo says, bowing and slobbering on her hand. He's fat and his eyes roam.

"Lorraine, actually," Maryse says. "I kept my birth name."

"My apologies, Ms. Lorraine!" he says, and slobbers on her hand again before he turns to me. "Western women!" he says. "I know that you have your hands full!"

We're in the state room at the Pink Palace, Government House, drinking martinis with about a hundred other guests in black tie and evening gowns. Maryse is wearing her one really formal outfit, a brilliant white floor-length dress that hangs from one shoulder and hugs her fine body in a riveting way. I try to steer her away from Alijo, but he's persistent.

"So you are new to our country?" he says, nominally to both of us but mostly to Maryse. He stands too close to her, and when she steps back he crosses the distance, and when she steps back again she bumps into a tuxedoed back. The man turns around and his expression turns from puzzlement to delight when he sees Maryse.

"Franja!" the minister says. "This is the new Canadian Second Secretary and his beautiful wife, Ms. Lorraine."

Now there are two fat, leering men pressing in on Maryse.

"Mr. Franja is a very wealthy fellow," the minister says, slurping his drink.

"Pleased to meet you, sir," I say, stepping in and offering my hand. To take it he has to turn his shoulder and give Maryse a little breathing room. He has thick eyebrows and a heavy mustache.

"And Mr. Alijo is a well-known scoundrel," says Franja.

"How do you make your money?" Maryse asks, ducking between the two of them and then grabbing my arm for protection, nearly spilling my drink. It's so hot in the room that the sweat seeps freely down my face. Franja and Alijo close in on Maryse.

"That is not always a safe question in this room!" Alijo says jovially, waving his drink suddenly in an expansive gesture to take in the whole scene. There are diplomats here from a number of countries, but mostly it's a showcase for the local *lumito,* whose cars, jewels, watches and dresses come from Europe, whose children are beautiful and cloistered, who live in walled villas protected by private guards, and who, most of all, make their appearances at the Pink Palace. Minitzh is supposed to be here, too, but I haven't seen him. The Santa Irenian women in the room, without exception, are dazzlingly beautiful, young and vibrant in sleek dresses, with glistening manes of black hair. Trophy women, Maryse calls them, no doubt the mistresses of the state ministers, businessmen and Minitzh relatives clotted here tonight.

"But it's a fair question," Franja says. "Ms. Lorraine is not some mindless island flower. You probably have a degree in economics or some such subject, am I right?"

"I'm an artist, actually," Maryse says.

"An artist?" says Franja, leaning in as if he can't see her unless their noses nearly touch. "Well, I have some pieces I must show you."

"Ah," Maryse says.

"And your husband, too, of course!" says Franja, without looking at me. "Watabi sculpture, in mahogany and teak. Very rare. Very voluptuous."

"Weren't the Watabi wiped out by the British?" I say.

"Decisively," says Franja. "Magnificently. Their art is now priceless." He takes a drink, his eyes never leaving Maryse's. "Of course, I'm joking," he says. "It was a disaster for the Watabi. But on the other hand there aren't any of them left now, so we have no Watabi problem. The British are a thorough people."

"I think I need to find the washroom," Maryse says.

"The Watabi were an artist race," Alijo says. "They grew rice and they made art. Mr. Franja has a fantastic collection."

"Excuse me," Maryse says. Franja doesn't move and so she must squeeze between them again to break free. As she leaves both Franja and Alijo stare until she's swallowed by the crowd.

"I think Western women are very spirited," Alijo says to me. "Like *artillo* — hot spices. Hard to manage, but exciting. Is that right?"

"Mr. Burridge is not going to discuss his wife in front of you!" Franja says. The minister looks at me quickly, as if to say, But she's gone. What's the problem?

"The women here," Franja says, crowding close to me, "are sweet as ripe fruit. You've come all the way across the world, you don't want to miss it. Someone in your position — there will be opportunities. There are things in life you'll want to taste."

"My pleasure would be short-lived," I say, as diplomatically as possible. "And my death would be gruesome."

"Like Bobbit?" Franja says, and the two of them laugh uproariously as he makes a slicing motion across his groin. "We had our own case of that," Alijo says, laughing and drinking. "It was in all our newspapers. You see, it won't be so long now until our fruit will be spoiled as well."

Maryse is not coming back and so thankfully the two lose interest in me. I talk for a while with a reporter from the government paper. Then there's a sudden flurry as people turn to see Minitzh arrive, but it isn't him, it's his cousin Tinto, a wiry, tiny man with a pocked face, wearing a white suit and surrounded by pretty young men who are supposed to be his security team. I look for Maryse but can't find her, and then the entertainment starts, a troop of about thirty *koyolo*, transvestite dancers who swirl about a silver stage in glittering high-slit dresses, their hair dressed with feathers and their faces coated in makeup. The reporter tells me the *koyolo* are more glamorous than even most Santa Irenian beauties, they've spent so much money on their implants and hormones, their clothes and jewels.

"They're Santa Irene's most high-priced prostitutes," he says.

"Why's that?"

"Because they're not really women," he says. "So God won't punish you for fucking them."

I find Maryse finally in a corridor outside the state room, leaning against a pillar, holding herself.

"Are you all right?" I ask.

"I have to go home."

In the taxi she says, "What are we doing here, Bill?"

"It's my job. It's just for a couple of years."

"I almost threw up in there," she says. "Those people are so corrupt it oozes out of them."

"Not all of them."

"You have such a gentle nature," she says. "You're either completely wrong to be a diplomat or absolutely perfect."

"What do you mean?"

"I mean, either you don't realize what's really going on and so are clued out, and thus absolutely wrong for the work. Or you do realize but forgive and gloss over, and thus absolutely right."

"I realize," I say.

"You realize, but you can still eat the frogs' legs and hobnob with the well-heeled scum of humanity."

"It's my job."

"It's your job, but you can do it. I get physically sick around those people. I'm never going back to that place."

"Are you all right?"

"My head is feeling freeze-dried."

"Did you bring your pills?"

"No."

"We'll be home soon."

"I don't think so," she says.

"What?"

"I don't think I will be home soon. Home is in Ottawa. This isn't it. This is — "

"Shhh."

"I don't think I can stay here two years."

"Let's not talk about it."

"I'm just telling you."

"I know."

She rests her head against my shoulder and the streets speed by, black and unlit. We could be in outer space, it feels so empty and cold.

Every day, once a day, and I never have the strength. This stupid goddamn will to live! Misguided, self-punishing. My torturers aren't out there, they're inside me. Pushing some distant core of my being to keep going. I don't understand it. Any of it. All I have to do is refuse the water, not have *linala*. Spit it out. A hunger strike. Fast unto peace. It wouldn't take long. I'm a wreck as it is. Everything hurts. My shoulders, ribs, skin, teeth, eyes, feet, legs, ass. Split open like a seed. Spilling myself out. I'm no good to anyone now. Not Maryse, not Patrick, no one. They've done the worst to me.

Why can't I die? It's got to be fundamental. Every animal knows. Leg caught in the trap, life oozing onto the snow. Wait and die. The teeth at your throat: a moment of peace. Struggle no more. Rest now, return to the worms.

There's no point any more in this struggle. Who's struggling? What force still gulps that water when it arrives? Not me. It isn't me. I don't want it. I don't!

Except I must have it. Even when it means what it means. Those bastards and their hard-on for the CIA. Fuck me! I will not think about it. I mustn't think about it.

Their breath and the sting of it and how suddenly I wanted to rip their balls off but I couldn't turn around and how they left me wailing on the dirt floor when all I wanted was a bullet and an end.

"And then they raped me."

I can see myself in the therapy group. There's a man there from Guatemala, a Sri Lankan Tamil, a Sikh somehow escaped from the Punjab police. A Chinese woman clutching her belly, talking about her dead baby. We're all here. It's a little corner of a church basement that doubles as a daycare on weekdays. We're sitting on tiny chairs in a circle, not looking at each other, and the woman leading the group is a white twenty-six year-old social worker in tennis shoes and pressed blue jeans and gold-rimmed glasses. Her sandy hair is braided. I see this all very clearly. The Tamil man is talking, his head bobbing. He's saying that he went to Colombo from the north to escape the Tamil Tigers but was picked up at a roadblock without identity documents. Where were his identity documents? He must have lost them in the morning. The refugee camps were full of people willing to steal someone's identity and sell it to the smugglers. The soldier unable to speak Tamil. What was he doing manning a roadblock in a Tamil area when he could only speak Sinhala?

This is real now. It feels real. I'm in this church basement room listening to the testimony of these torture survivors. I'm among them. Which means I survived. It's over. I made it! If you wait long enough, everything comes to an end! I've nothing to worry about any more!

"And then they raped me," he says in his little singsong voice, his eyes down. We all lower our eyes at the same time, except the social worker — her eyes go up. She makes a note on her clipboard. There's a long silence. It suddenly feels uncomfortable. Is that it? Is his story over? That means someone else will have to talk. If you want to join the group you have to talk. Even I know that.

But it isn't over. "How many were there, Linga?" the social

worker asks. Her voice sharp as glass. She shouldn't be allowed to graduate with a voice like that.

"Five, I think," Linga says, rubbing his thighs back and forth now. The Guatemalan is staring at a spot on the floor, his lips pressed together.

"How long did it last?"

"I think, maybe, twenty minutes," he says, then shakes his head. "Perhaps it was two hours."

"And how did that make you feel?'

She has her pen in her hand, and it's the first time really I want to grab a little daycare chair and smash it across her head. *How did that make you feel?* There's suddenly no air in the room. I need to get up and walk away. I need to, but my legs don't work very well. I stay where I am. Think again: This is all so real it must mean I've escaped. It's here and now. I can't remember the details, don't want to remember the details. *I made it out.* That's all that's important.

The social worker leans in toward Linga. "How did that make you feel?" she asks again.

"Very bad," he says.

She writes that down on her paper, as if somehow he has told her something she didn't know.

"Everything seems so normal," Maryse says. We're walking with Patrick on the wall of Fort Browning, which looks down on Santa Irene from the western ridge. There are patches of other tourists — a lot of Japanese gentlemen in baseball caps, some Australians, a couple speaking German. "Polluted, but normal," she says.

There's a brown haze. When you live in it it's easy to forget about it, but up here you can see the blue sky above the brown.

The sea shimmers grey and large in the distance, and on the eastern ridge the Pink Palace is just a blotch of odd colour.

"Daddy! A spider!" Patrick points to the edge of a gun mounting where a yellow and black beauty has set up shop. We're seeing them everywhere these days, on webs stretched between telephone lines and dangling from street lamps, shadowed like black hands against the sky. Patrick goes off to find an unlucky ant and Maryse squeezes my hand.

"I keep thinking of what Peter said about the corpses on the beaches," she says.

"Well, I think *most* of the life here really is normal," I say. "You get used to the checkpoints, right?"

"They're not checking diplomats too closely."

"No, they're not. But I haven't seen too many people having troubles. It all seems pretty routine."

"And we don't read it in the news and it never gets on TV and people don't want to talk about it," she says. "But if you happen to get in trouble you're liable to end up in the harbour with your body slit."

"There are a lot of countries like this," I say. "In fact, maybe most countries are like this. Nobody knows how many people are in labour camps in China. Some official has it in for you and you could end up raking rocks the rest of your life. But millions of other people run around like crazy buying refrigerators and stereos and investing in phony stocks and paying off local officials. It's just life. Life is big. There's room for the terrible, and there's room for the wonderful."

"I can't believe you just said that," she says.

"What?"

"Doesn't this appall you? They're rounding up kids from the villages. We're living in the middle of it like spoiled tourists."

"Diplomats," I say. "It's a special status. We're not here to change this country. Not directly. We observe and we represent, and at all times we stand a little apart because that's the role."

"That's *your* role."

"Yes. My role."

We've been through some of this before. Maryse would like to do some NGO work, which would be good, but I've told her she can't get too involved in promoting social change. And not involved at all in human rights, I would think, but I'll have to talk to Peter about that.

Patrick has stopped looking for ants, his attention diverted to some black pebbles near the base of the wall. I squat down to look at them with him for a while, then he says, "Daddy, why there are guns?" He means the cannons pointing out at the harbour.

"They're to protect the city from invaders," I say.

"But Daddy, why there are *guns*?"

"Well, you can imagine in the olden days a navy sailing into this harbour. All those ships have cannons on them, and the cannons are blasting away, and the buildings in the town are getting hit by cannon balls. That would be terrible, wouldn't it? Well, these big cannons here," I say, standing up and pointing to them, "they'd be bigger than the cannons on the ships. And from up on a height like this, they could send cannon balls way into the harbour. So they could hit enemy ships before the enemy ships could hit the town."

Patrick concentrates on the black pebbles as the explanation gets more complicated.

I look out at the harbour again. "This would be a nice scene to paint," I say.

"I'm sorry, it disgusts me," Maryse says, and I wait for her joke but there isn't one. Finally I say, "Well, it's disgusting, in a way, but mostly it just *is*. It's life, human life, and force — violence — is a really strong part of it. Part of our history, part of our present, part of our future certainly. So many of the important events of the past turned on violence, on armies, acts of war, sabotage. Treaties signed to avoid violence. We all deplore it but it won't go away.

Saddam Hussein invades Kuwait and George Bush turns Iraq into a parking lot. In Canada we feel that kind of thing doesn't pertain to us, things have been so peaceful most of the time. But for a lot of the world it's a daily reality. Here we have a privileged position, we get to avoid it, really, view reality without getting stuck in the swamp. You could set up your paints here and make a painting that captured the whole sweep of this view — the grime and the pollution and the ghosts of old violence and the new violence lurking, and that silly Pink Palace and the big ocean just out there gleaming and huge enough to drown all this without a ripple. Make a painting like that so people see clearly. That would be worth several months of NGO work and maybe a lot more. Make use of what's here in front of you. That's what an artist does."

"How the fuck do you know what an artist does?" she says, but gently, taking both of my hands.

"I'm married to one."

It isn't the end of the discussion, but Patrick is bored so we move on. In the gift shop we buy a dozen assorted postcards of famous Santa Irenian sites, including this fort, and the *Emerald*, which was sunk in the harbour in 1942 and pulled up about ten years ago to be converted into a seafood restaurant, and the largest Catholic church in the hemisphere, St. Basil's, made of white Italian marble hauled into the jungle a four-hour ride from the capital.

In the taxi, stuck in traffic, with Patrick squirming between us, Maryse takes my hand and says, "Don't tell me what to paint, all right?"

"Sorry?"

"You've brought me all the way out here, where I'm completely dependent on you, and I'm trying my best to fit into the corset of this new life. I appreciate your positive nature, and you know I love you very much. But don't tell me what to paint."

"Daddy!" Patrick says.

"Shhh, sweetie," Maryse says. "Daddy and I are talking."

"But you're always talking!" Patrick says.

"No we're not. Not always," she says.

"Daddy," Patrick asks. "Why there are guns?"

Hands reaching. Jerked awake so suddenly I try to kick out, wrench my back. Still bound and hooded. Head slammed against something hard, concrete floor maybe, then I'm being carried. Feels like on someone's shoulder. Quickly. Voices loud, urgent. Doors slamming. Running, running, then someone drops me, screams something in Kuantij. Leave me, I think. Just leave me. Save yourselves. Go!

But they pick me up. Several hands. Voices. Josef's among them. He's the calmest.

Dumped now. In a trunk. Door slamming, engine starting. Are those shots? I huddle instinctively, waiting for the gas tank to ignite. Death now. In a second from now. Waiting, expecting. *The hostage was killed in the raid.* Probable outcome. If the IS are involved.

The car accelerates suddenly. We roar off and I wait for the crash, know it's going to happen. There's nowhere to drive in the capital without running into traffic. At this speed we're going to crash into something. Maybe I'll die. Maybe I won't.

Could I walk out of here? Not strong enough. Getting there. Might survive. Not impossible.

The crash doesn't come. No tires are shot out. We don't slam into anything, but roar on until I wonder, Where the hell are we? How could they keep going at this speed and not run into something in the worst traffic on the face of the planet?

Nothing. A clean break. I don't know how long we drive. Seems like an hour, maybe more. But I can't keep track of time, don't know if days or minutes are going by. Trying to stay alert but a vagueness clouds almost everything. Have to fight it. Have to keep alive who I am. Where. Who I've been.

When they pull me out the air feels cooler somehow, even in the hood, not so stifling. Different sounds. Not traffic sounds, not city. They've brought me to the mountains, I think.

This could be my chance. If I can get stronger. Stay patient. There will be a chance. Might be. If I stay alert.

They put me again in a small place but it smells different, feels different. When my heart slows and the cigarettes go away I hear the throbbing of cicadas.

"Is this a village?" I ask Josef. They've pulled me onto the floor and someone — it must be Josef — is feeding me through the mouth hole in my hood. *Linala.* It's all I've eaten. For how long? As long as I've been captured. Maybe a couple of months or more. How can I still be alive?

Coughing coughing coughing. I thought I was over that. But it's back, bad as ever. I need real food. Vitamins. Something to re-build my body.

"Is this a village?" I ask again. Then keeping my mouth open, waiting for the spoon. Like an animal.

"Eed," says Josef. I feel the ache of this slight nourishment glid-ing into me.

"I need light," I say. "Josef. Please. Take off the hood."

More food. More food and more food.

"Please Josef. Take off the hood."

His answer is a sudden kick in the chest. It's so unexpected I topple and cry out, the *linala* spilling from my lips and into my hood.

I wait for more. When kicks come they usually don't stop at one. If I huddle and stay low then maybe they won't last too long.

Nothing. I wait. Moss on a rock. Through seasons. Still. No more.

"Josef," I say from the floor. Dirt. We must be in a village. "I need light. You're going to blind me. If you want to keep me alive, don't hack me off piece by piece."

Silence.

"Josef, for God's sake, you know by now I'm not the CIA. I'm not the IS. You don't have to do this to me."

Waiting. Silence. Footsteps leaving. Then someone picking me up by the arms, dumping me back in my hole where the mosquitoes have free access. They attack at all hours, stinging my hands and wrists and ankles, sometimes even getting inside my hood and biting my eyelids, cheeks, temples. When I'm awake I roll my head constantly and rub my wrists and hands. The skin is raw and cut from the rope. Probably infected. I don't want to think about it. I'm already beleaguered by shaking and chills — probably malaria. Asleep, I just get eaten. I'm asleep most of the time now. Not enough food to stay awake.

Flex and relax, flex and relax. Still trying to keep control of some of my muscles. Have to stay alert at least some of the time. Escape not impossible, only if I can't move.

Walking at all would be a marathon now, I think.

The army doesn't like to patrol in the villages. How do I know that? I just do. Peter must've told me. But they do patrol. That must be why they never take off my hood. This isn't a safe spot for them to keep me.

So I must stay alert. Be ready if a chance comes up. You never know. It's not impossible.

Stay alert. Flex and relax. And stay who you are. That's the hard thing. Because I'm going to walk down that road at some point and Patrick and Maryse are going to be there. I don't want to be human garbage. Can't let this erase everything else. Just can't.

Why the fuck am I thinking this way? A bullet to the brain — release finally. Patrick and Maryse won't have to deal with this sack of shit. With me. I don't want to survive this. Don't want them to find my body. Not like this. This isn't me. I stopped being me when they picked me up. That's the day I died, this is just a lingering hell. God and the devil ganging up, a tag-team, the torturer and the cheerleader.

Breathing. Sores inside my mouth. Chills and coughs. Gaps for teeth. Everything in pain. Be still. Still as a lizard on a rock. Still as a rock *under* a lizard. Dead and insensitive. Cold and unmoving. Unfeeling. The best thing. Unfeeling and without pain. Here's my prayer to the almighty duo: turn me into rock, seep my blood into soil. Peace of the worms. Peace of the worms. Peace of the fucking worms.

Cigarettes again. I sweat the second I smell them. Voices. Low, not laughing the way they usually do. Can't make out any particular words. Little streams of muddy words. Undercurrents. Why the fuck haven't I learned any Kuantij yet? I've been so useless, rotting here. Mind fading off all the time. Visiting. Useless visiting. Mental masturbation. I could have been concentrating.

Footsteps. Coming closer. Oh shit. No. *No!* Please God. Fuck God. God or the devil. The both of you! Don't bring them here. I'm a bag of shit, painful shit. I know they can bring more pain. I know they can. Don't let them do it. Don't. Stop them, please, I beg you, both of you. Damn you!

Silence. But still the cigarettes. They're standing right in front of me, I don't know how many. Could be five. Could be only one. Can feel the heat of their breath. Oh shit. Oh shit oh shit oh shit oh shit! I took everything. They did everything to me and I took it and I'm still here stupidly stupidly I should have died I should've why didn't I die? Why not? It's not fair. Anybody else would've died. Anybody.

This goddamn silence. I can't stand it. I can't! They're just standing, I can feel them, can smell the smoke and hate. Smoke and hate. Reeking from them. Can't see but man I can smell these bastards, hear the hate molecules banging in their brains.

Have to be still. Maybe they think I'm dead. I'm breathing but the air passes in so slowly my lungs don't move, chest still, might be random movement of air. That's how still I've learned to be. Still as a lizard on a rock. As a rock under a lizard. They won't move, I won't move. Rocks, all of us. No one gets hurt as rocks. That's the good thing about rocks.

Shut up, brain! In all this shit I've learned to keep everything still but my brain. Brain just keeps chattering. Like they can't hear it. Like every moment's got to be filled with some kind of mental noise. Shut up!

Shhh. Quiet. They're being quiet, I'll be quiet. Soft heart. That's the other raging part. Hammer hammer hammer. Heart knows what these fuckers do. Heart knows it, runs as if it can get away. Hammer hammer hammer. Little rabbit heart. Still. Damn. Still.

Like a rock under a lizard. Hardening. Crack a rock, crush a rock, split it, no pain. Slowly weathered grain by grain, doesn't matter. Rock feels nothing. Cold, hot, starving, doesn't matter. Crush me for gravel, see what I care!

Shhh. Quiet. They can be quiet, I can be . . .

"Boo-reej."

Damn! I move my head, gasp, heart slams slams slams. The sound of my name burning into my brain. I lose it. Meant to be still. Couldn't stand it.

"What the fuck!" I yell, loud as I can, my voice startling me, painful, alarming. *"What the fuck do you want? What are you doing to me? Fuck fuck fuckers!"* Writhing, trying to kick at them, out of

control. Hands shackled, legs don't go very far anyway, and oh, it hurts, this sudden movement. Want to catch one of them in the balls just once. But no, I barely know where my foot is.

They start laughing. Sounds like eight, ten, a hundred of them. A whole house packed with them. I can't stand it. Just shoot me, you fuckers! I try kicking again, they laugh but their feet move out of the way. Now I'm in for it. Face first into the shit. They're laughing and I'm entertainment. Oh shit! Why couldn't I have just stayed still?

Laughing, talking, taunting. Throwing my name at me like rotten fruit. "Boo-reej! Boo-reej! Boo-reej!" I can't stand it. I can't take any more if it.

"Shoot me!" I scream, the words scraping my throat like razors. *"Assholes! End it! Now! Shoot me! Shoot me!"* Then I'm crying, gasping, choking on the hood. Not enough air. I have to calm down for air. But I don't want air. A minute of this, that's all. Then I'm free. Free as a fucking rock. Just a minute. Please! I jerk my head, trying to increase the choke. Trying. I can do it this time. I can. I know it.

No laughter now. Hands on my head, pulling it back. I can't choke myself anyway. It's very cleverly done. To a point but not over. To pain but not death. Not rest. Never rest.

Hands pulling. Then something hard to my temple. I'm so slow. It takes me so long. It's a gun barrel. My reaction horrifies me. When I know.

"No! Oh no, please no!" I scream. It must be me, that voice from in here, from in the hood. Must be mine. From the basement of my soul. The lowest reaches. Where maggots feed on rats.

More time. More time! It's so stupid but there it is. I want more time but I'm not going to get it. A moment after I recognize the feel of the gun it goes off, louder than I can imagine. Everything freezes to a scream but it's not what I expect at all, not anything like it. I scream and scream long after the shot, scream down into hell, exactly where I've been all along, nothing different, it's so strange. Until I realize they fired beside my ear, but it's hours and hours exploding in my brain, won't end, rage without let-up. That I wanted more of! Spineless little shit.

Bone. It's all I have left. Rigid, fleshless, jutting bone. Man of bone. Breathing bone. Breathing man of bone.

Hood off, shackles off, in the dark with the maggots and the mosquitoes, with my chills and aches, my brain going yammer yammer yammer. And these bones. Long, skeletal, wrapped in bags of deflated skin. Where there used to be muscles. Used to be sinews and what else? Flesh. I had flesh before. It wasn't discoloured like this crumply skin, with burn marks and bruises and running sores. My beard so itchy. A clever person would be able to tell from this beard how long they've held me. This is no svelte little beard. This is a months-long, lifetime kind of beard.

Of course. That's how long: a lifetime. Several lifetimes. A month of Sundays. Ages since I've seen you. Rip van Winkle. Twenty years?

Yammer yammer yammer.

Man of bone. Why can't I just make my brain still? That would be a consolation. *They captured me, but I learned to meditate. Actually, it was one of the most peaceful periods of my life.*

The thought is so ridiculous I start laughing. Strange, giddy, sobbing, painful laughter. I must have some broken ribs. It hurts so much. My ear still echoing like an ocean from the gunshot. When was that?

Shoulderblades and jutting hips and ribcage stark against this bag of skin. Cheekbones, elbows, huge knobbly knees. Man of bone. Like Auschwitz. Like the Hong Kong prisoners. I remember the pictures. Those stark men of bone with the large blank eyes, trousers held up with ropes. Not blank eyes, no — a different kind of wisdom. From the reaches of hell.

Here I am in the reaches of hell, indestructable man of bone. They can't kill me. *I can't be killed!* No, nothing so simple. I can be starved, beaten, shocked, humiliated, kicked, taunted, degraded, ground into gravel and taken away by the shovelful. But I can't be *killed!* I cannot die. Man of bone for all time, doomed and cursed to suffer with my eyes open.

Why do I keep my eyes open? Because I'm a man of bone. I'm supposed to see it all.

"There is a word for it in Punjabi," the Sikh says. Back in the basement in the daycare. Our little circle of survivors. How could I imagine this? It doesn't have the feel of a dream, doesn't quite seem a memory. It's the bloody microchip. They programmed me to *know* I'll survive.

But that's not true either. The CIA wouldn't go to the trouble of inventing a separate life. They'd just put a little bomb in your head. Hi-tech cyanide. Much more cost-effective.

It's God who's doing this, God and the devil. Stringing me along. Hope springs eternal. It's a fucking conspiracy. Trying to make me believe my life has been worthwhile. I shouldn't cooperate. But I'm a spineless shit. I know that now. I'll know it the rest of my days. This voice unstoppable.

"We call it the *ghotna*. It's a heavy log, used for crushing grain. Where I come from, you know, we are all farmers. They lay you out on the floor and roll the *ghotna* on your legs, especially your thighs. One police stands on one end and another on the other and they roll your muscles flat. I cannot tell you what it feels like.

It obliterates everything else. You can feel yourself becoming a cripple."

He sits straight in his little chair, his turban royal blue, beard dark as his eyes.

"If you think about it, it's such an extraordinary thing to do, because they say they are looking for information, to make you talk. But you cannot talk while they are rolling the *ghotna* over you. You cannot talk, you cannot think, pain is everything. You black out most of the time. How are you supposed to be thinking of the names of terrorists, of people you know? Not a thought can get in edgewise!"

His smile almost charismatic, teeth and eyes so bright.

"How did you make it through?" the social worker asks. Again she has her pen poised. This is all going into some doctoral thesis. She wants to get the words right.

"*Waheguru*," he says, smiling.

"What?"

"Whenever they brought out the *ghotna*, or stretched my legs so wide apart, or humiliated me, I said in my mind over and over, '*Waheguru, Waheguru, Waheguru.*'"

"What's that?" the social worker asks.

"Well," he says, smiling, as if it's obvious. "It is the name of my God."

How can I see this in such detail? The social worker writing things down. She has a name. What is it? If I were really here I would know her name. I would know how I got here. Did I drive? Did someone pick me up? I would know what I'm going to do after the session is over. Go home, go to bed, drink myself stupid, slash my wrists? Turn on the television. I would know. But it seems real right now. It seems like an escape of sorts. I don't want to think about it too closely. It's better here than in the hood.

The Chinese woman speaks next. Her English is halting. We are all pitching in soon, and I know a little Chinese. How do I know that? From a past life. I used to study China. I used to make my tongue chop out those little syllables. *Hao jile!* Somewhere in my brain they're still stored.

She tells us about going to the countryside to stay with her aunt after she got pregnant. Staying inside, cooking over the little charcoal stove for the whole family. Sleeping on a mat on the floor, all of them in the one room. Then hearing that the family planners from her work unit had discovered where she was, were coming to find her. Rushing out just minutes before their truck pulled up. Hiding in the rice paddy overnight, emerging cold and nearly unconscious, covered in leeches. Sick by the stove, shivering on her mat. Thinking she'd lost the baby. Her husband coming to find her. No, I will not come back! I've suffered too much to stop now.

Then three weeks before she's due, another birth control squad shows up, this time from the neighbouring township. Midnight, no warning, bursting through the door of the hut, shining their flashlights. All pregnant women into the van! Clutching her blanket. No! Screaming no!

Bouncing down the rutted road. The long drive. Sobbing. Clutching at her belly. The beginnings of labour. "Stop it! You must hang on!" they screamed at her. Running her on a stretcher through the hospital. Knocking people over. The baby coming. The baby! It's a girl. Another girl. Reaching out her arms to her baby. The one embrace, then she's taken off, not even wrapped in a blanket. "Wrap her please — she's alive!" Pleading, crying, then the afterbirth. No strength. No way left to fight.

The long bus trip back to her husband later. Her eyes unfocused. Clutching her bag with the tin of hot rice, the thermos of tea. Not having any of it. Not deserving. Her body so dead yet so sore.

This is not the place I want to go for refuge, I think. It feels real but it isn't real. It's some place invented in my brain. But it's not the place I want to go.

I don't seem to have any choice. The Guatemalan is talking now. A shrunken man, Gomez, a doctor. He speaks in quiet, slow sentences. I don't want to hear them but I don't have any choice. "I was picked up on a main street in broad daylight in Guatemala city," he says, hardly a hint of emotion. "A white van with polarized windows. I was so slow. I thought they were coming for somebody else. I heard my name, Luis Gomez, turned and there was already a hand on the back of my neck. I started to speak and then my head slammed into the pavement. Everyone was watching. There must have been a hundred people. No one did a thing. My hands were tied, they shoved me head first into a burlap bag, they threw me in the back of the van."

On the wall above Gomez is a daily activity chart for the preschoolers. I try to concentrate on the rounded, feminine writing. Monday 8:30–10:15: supervised free play. 10:15–10:30: snack time — fruit cups with pita bread and juice. 10:30–11:00: circle time. I'm focusing above Gomez's head because I don't want to hear his words.

"I could smell gasoline. On my face I felt the steel grooves on the floor of the van. Time and again we stopped, the doors opened, someone else in a burlap bag landed on top of me. I could hear their moans, smell their blood. Always the same angry voices, calling us sympathizers, *comunistas*. My father was a communist. He was killed in 1954. I have treated some *campesinos*, that is all. The way I would treat anyone who came to my office."

11:00–11:30: creative art. 11:30–12:00: supervised free play.

"We drove for what seemed like hours. It was dark when we stopped. There was dust in the van. The heat was unbearable. All these bodies on top of me. Some still breathing, I could feel them. Some not. I was too scared to talk. I guess the others were as well, the ones still alive. The van stopped, the doors opened, one of the bags was pulled out. I could hear them pushing, rolling, dragging the body off the road. Then there was a gunshot, two, three. Then laughter and a strange hissing noise. They were pissing on the body. They'd been drinking beer in the front of the van and now every time they stopped, dragged someone out and shot him, they pissed on the body as well."

12:00–12:45: I can't make it out. It must be lunch. The next segment is hidden by Gomez's greying hair. He's looking at me all the time he speaks. I don't want to look at him.

"They stopped then outside a bar. I could hear the sounds of music inside, and the three of them talking in the front. Should we kill the last ones, then get drunk, or get drunk now and kill them later? They couldn't decide. I soiled my pants listening to them. Their voices got louder and louder. It sounded like someone had brought out his gun, was waving it at the others. Good, I thought, shoot each other, *hijueputa!* But they decided in the end to get drunk. I heard them stumbling down the road away from the van. I don't know where my brain was. It took me so long to remember the knife in my pocket. There were still two or three bodies piled on top of me. I whispered at them but there was no reply. They were dead or unconscious or too afraid to make a sound. But I managed to find my knife, to cut my way out of the burlap bag. It was the hardest thing of my whole life, cutting my way out from beneath those bodies. In my heart of hearts I knew it was too late. The bastards were coming back. They'd catch me on my way out, shoot me right there on the side of the road. It wouldn't matter who saw. Bodies were common then. Everyone knew of someone who had disappeared.

"I knew they'd get me. But they were too drunk! I made it out the side door just as they were walking back but they didn't even hear the slam when I closed it. I just made it to the bushes when they drove away."

2:15–3:00: naptime. 3:00–3:30: story time. 3:30–4:30: supervised free play. 4:30–5:30: pickup by parents. Friday is laundry day. Duty parents must find a replacement laundry family if they are unable to take the laundry.

"So you see I was never tortured. I got a bump on the head which healed quickly. Yet I cannot close my eyes without that van driving up to me again. I hear my name and it's always too late: Luis Gomez! I think of those others in the bags I did nothing to help. On their way to be shot and dumped and pissed on. Me hiding in the bushes with shit in my pants. Every time I close my eyes I am there again. Nine years and I still have nightmares! And I am a doctor, so I know every drug to erase this type of pain. There is none. It does not get erased."

The social worker scribbling down his testimony as if she'll be tested on it later in the term. Why don't I know her name? If this is happening for real then I'd know her name. But it isn't real, it's my brain trying to skip ahead. Skip, go, do it! Anywhere but here.

It's my turn to talk but the daycare turns blurry. The children are coming back. It isn't time for the trauma relief group. Our time is over. It hasn't come yet. It's not going to come. I know all these characters. They've been served up by my brain. Snippets of things I've read, stirred together into some imaginary soup. This never happened. It's not going to happen. Hope only brings more pain. I know that. I know.

In my dream there's a fire and Graham and I are trying to get out the upstairs window but we can't lift it open. We keep straining and straining and the smoke fills up the room but the window won't open. Graham says we have to break it but I say no, we're not allowed, so we try some more. It gets hotter and Graham starts to cry and I look around for something to use to open the window. Graham shouts, "Just break it!" but we can't, we're not allowed.

Then I wake up and smell smoke, so I go downstairs in my pajamas. I walk toward the light in the kitchen. It's winter and the floor is cold on my bare feet. Dad is sitting in his bathrobe at the kitchen table, smoking, reading a book. I've never seen him smoking before and at first I think I must still be dreaming. The light is funny — it isn't the warm light of the lamp on the table but the cold fluorescent light from over the stove.

"You should go back to bed, Billy."

"What are you doing, Daddy?"

"Just go back to bed."

"Smoking will kill you!"

"Just go back to bed," he says. He uses his hard voice that means what it says but I can't move. It's as if I've come down the stairs to find this stranger pretending to be my father.

"Do you want some warm milk?" he asks finally, and he's my father again. He takes his cigarette over to the sink and runs water over it. The wet ashes have a sharp smell.

"I had a bad dream," I say, and while he's heating the milk I tell him about it. "Dreams are funny," he says when I'm finished.

When the milk is ready I sit at the table with him and he reads some more. It's a thick book with a golden cover showing an almost naked woman who has a knife sticking out of her chest. I sip my milk and notice the lines on his face, the grey in the whiskers that make his face so scratchy to kiss, how tired his eyes look. The clock on the stove says 1:24. When I'm nearly finished he puts down his book and says, "At some point in every man's life, he comes to the conclusion that his wife is crazy."

I finish my milk and look at him.

"Just remember this, Billy. At some point you're going to conclude —"

"I'm not getting married," I say.

"Every man says that, too. Then after they do get married they reach this conclusion. It doesn't necessarily happen soon. It could take years. All I'm telling you is at some point — "

He repeats himself and I nod because he wants me to remember

this for the rest of my life, even though I don't know what he's talking about. It's one of those adult things you only understand a bit
of.

"The other thing," he says, "is about shoulders. Every man has
to have big shoulders." I raise my shoulders and he reaches over to
flatten them again. "What I mean by that," he says, "is you have to
bear up. Let things run off you like water. Have big shoulders.
Take the responsibility. Be big about things. Don't hold grudges.
Carry the load. Be a gentleman. Have big shoulders. Do you know
what I mean?"

I nod again even though I don't.

"You see, women are on cycles. They go up and down all the
time. When you get married you'll come to understand. You can
graph them out if you want. At certain times of the month they're
just going to be crazy. As a man, what you have to do is accept
that. Shrug your shoulders. Let it wash off. She'll be normal again
by next week. Whatever normal is. Have big shoulders. That's
what you're there for."

My feet are getting cold and I have to go the bathroom, but I
don't want to leave. There's more that he wants to tell me and he
won't want to say it in the daytime.

He says, "Men get crazy, too, but it's not the same. You'll understand this when you're older. A man gets crazy till he realizes and
accepts that his wife is crazy. Once you accept it it gets better. You
can wait it out, cook dinner for her, buy some flowers. Do you
have to have a pee?"

"No," I say.

"Yes, you do," he says. "You should go back to bed, too. Don't
tell your mother anything about this conversation."

"Okay."

I slip off my chair and carry my mug to the sink, then run back
upstairs. The floor is so cold, especially in the bathroom. In my
room I put some socks on and pull the blankets over me and wriggle

in bed until the sheets are warm. Downstairs I can smell the smoke of another cigarette, but I can't stay awake long enough to tell my father again that it's bad.

"You did *what?*" Marlene the Australian vegetarian asks, and the plate that was resting on her knees suddenly tips over, dumping mango slices on the floor. There's confusion while she fusses about picking them up, and Maryse runs to the kitchen to ask Frita for a cloth, and Patrick laughs because anytime somebody else makes a mess it's funny. Frita comes out like a bowling ball, low to ground and authoritative, homing in on the disaster. She speaks only a few words of English and cooks with blistering spices. In just a couple of days she has taken over our lives.

"*Baba* Patrick, *yot!*" she says, shooing him away, and then gets on her knees and wipes furiously. She's round and sturdy and utterly focused. Marlene says something to her in Kuantij but Frita doesn't seem to hear. In a moment the area is sanitized, and then Frita withdraws to the kitchen and re-appears almost instantly with another plate of mango slices for Marlene.

"*Li-li*," Marlene says, the short form for thank-you to servants and younger people. The more formal, for superiors, is *nyo-li*. There, I'm learning a little.

"I'm sorry," Marlene says, taking an obligatory bite of mango before Frita will withdraw again. "You spilled *water* all over her?"

We're back to the old story of how Maryse and I got together. I glance out the window in slight embarrassment and notice the sun is dipping low. Late afternoon. It'll be dark by six o'clock.

"Not all over her," Maryse says, delighting in the retelling. "I caught the edge of the table and then it splashed on her lap."

"It was all down her front," I say.

"Mostly her legs," Maryse says.

"She had on a very smart suit and Maryse tipped the water pitcher all over her."

"It was an accident," she says.

"From where I was sitting," I say, "it looked deliberate."

"And she was gorgeous?" Marlene interjects.

"She was *too* pretty," Maryse says. I stay silent and Maryse turns on me. "She was, wasn't she?"

"He isn't saying." Marlene laughs.

"She was extraordinary," I say.

"Oh, you'd have been miserable!" Maryse says, scooping up a bit of mango with her fingers. In the heat and humidity her skin is rich and her hair looks wild and flourishing. "She was this hothouse creature who couldn't go outside without wearing makeup. Honestly. And Bill was the fifth man I saw her with in that coffee shop."

"Well, wait a minute," Marlene says, and Patrick interrupts her, wanting to go outside.

"Go get your hat on," I tell him.

"Daddy, come with me," he says.

"I'm going to stay here and make sure that history is properly recounted," I say.

"Daddy, come with me!" he says. Frita emerges then and takes him by the hand, chattering at him in Kuantij. She can barely understand us but always seems to know what's needed.

"I'm just trying to get myself in the scene," Marlene says. "Maryse is the waitress, and she dumps water on this woman — "

"*Elaine*," Maryse says, doing her funny thing with the word, making her sound ridiculous and perfect at the same time.

"On Elaine, whose lonely hearts ad Bill had answered because he thought you were a lesbian . . ."

"That was so stupid of you," Maryse says.

"You had so many girlfriends — " I say.

"And then what happened?"

"I apologized. I fell all over myself apologizing," Maryse says.

"And what did Elaine do?"

"She couldn't handle it," Maryse says.

"She was very gracious," I say.

"She just fell apart," Maryse says. "Face it. If she couldn't look immaculate, she just dissolved."

"She didn't dissolve," I say.

"Oh, *Elaine*," she says, to show that this is a high joke between us. In fact there's more. It's a matter of marital conviction that Maryse saved me from a doomed romance with this woman. Subscription to any other view on this matter is not tolerated, in public or in private.

"Bill idealizes her," Maryse says, still joking-serious.

"I do not," I say.

"She was perfect. He had no time to discover any of her flaws. In fact, he might have been married to her for decades and not have discovered them. It's a good thing for me!"

"Quite right!" Marlene says.

"She was very gracious," I say slowly, and Marlene laughs.

"He's serious now," she says. "He can't joke about Elaine, even six years later."

"What I remember most," I say, "was her expression. Just at the moment when the water started to hit her. She didn't look at you at all. She looked across at me, with an expression of complete bewilderment — *What is the world doing to me now?* It's hard to explain, but I thought at the time it was the most human expression I'd ever seen. Think of it — here's this beautiful lady — "

"Too beautiful," Maryse says. But I don't want to joke about it. I want to explain it. Once and for all.

"Quite a beautiful lady," I say, not looking at Maryse. "And in this weird situation of meeting men who've responded to an ad in the paper. I'm sure they were all kind of like me — you hope the other person is going to be attractive, but then she turns out — "

"She gets more beautiful as the years go by," Maryse says.

"And she didn't really know much about me," I say, ignoring the danger signals, wanting to say the words anyway. "She didn't even know who I was, what I did, the most basic things. I didn't realize it at the time — "

"Bill thinks about her a lot," Maryse says.

" — but she was trying to fit herself into possible worlds. These men that she was meeting represented a way out of, I guess, the boredom of her situation. She was a junior accountant. Everybody in her office was married and boring. I got the sense that she hadn't been exposed to many possibilities — "

"Until Sir Galahad here arrived — "

"And then here I am sitting across from her, and I tell her that I work in the foreign service, and this whole new realm emerges in front of her eyes: traveling to other countries, stepping inside the *National Geographic*. It was like a paradigm shift. I thought I could see it in her eyes. And then there's this water jug being poured onto her lap, and this look in her eyes: *Where does this fit in?* "

"I nearly killed myself apologizing," Maryse says.

"But what happened?" Marlene asks.

"She went home," I say.

"She couldn't handle a little water," Maryse says.

"Her blouse was drenched," I say. "I could see her bra through it."

"You could not," Maryse says.

"White. Very lacy," I say.

"Large cup, too, I bet," says Maryse. "You didn't miss a thing."

Marlene sits between us, watching a married couple pretend not to fight over the roots of their romance.

"It was a memorable moment," I say.

"But how did you leave it?" Marlene asks.

"Elaine was going to call me," I say. "But she didn't call."

"She couldn't handle a little water," Maryse says again. "She'd never have made a diplomatic wife. Right, Bill?"

"Right, Maryse."

"And did you two sit talking for hours after she left?" Marlene asks.

"No, I left soon after as well," I say.

"But you called Maryse?"

"I figured anyone who would dump a gallon of ice water on a lady's lap just to get my attention — "

There's no time to finish because the world is suddenly washed with rain and Patrick and Frita rush in, Patrick screaming with the fun of it, his T-shirt plastered against his tiny ribs.

"Blast!" Marlene says. "I'd meant to be home by now. You people are just too interesting."

"Then you'll have to stay for dinner," Maryse says.

Stay for dinner. Stay in this place, this thought. Don't want to go back. Don't. Please no. Don't want to go back.

"Mr. Punjo? Is there a William Punjo here?" I scan the waiting room, packed as usual with various family groups who've come with their tin boxes full of food, their baskets, their children, their grandmothers who sit so still watching everything that happens.

"I am Edward Punjo," says a young man, perhaps in his twenties, with a bad scar on his neck and a ripped blue shirt and old black pants stained with red mud.

"The name I have for this appointment is William Punjo," I say.

"I am Edward Punjo," he says again.

"Is there a *William* Punjo here?" I ask the group. Lila comes out into the hall then and asks the question in Kuantij. She then has a long conversation with the young man and starts to show him into the interview room. I stop them both.

"Is this William Punjo?" I ask her.

"He's the cousin," Lila says.

"You know what Peter said about this," I say. "We're not accepting relatives anymore in the place of the actual person who's supposed to have the interview."

"This man says that William is dead," Lila says. "He says that he wants to claim asylum."

We sit around the brown table by the window and I let the young man talk. Lila takes notes and then summarizes for me. She says, "He claims he is from a village in Killusha district, called Oguntja. He was a peasant farmer there until the Kartouf came into his area. They recruited all the young men to join them and fight against the government. His cousin — William — joined them and became a squad commander. But this man did not want to join because it would have meant leaving his mother alone with four young children. His father was sick and died two years ago. He says that while William was a squad commander he could convince the Kartouf not to force him into service. But last month William was arrested by the IS and his body was just found washed up on the beach. So now Edward is afraid the Kartouf will come to recruit him in the village, and the IS will come to catch him in the city."

"How did you get the wound on your neck?" I ask. When Lila translates Edward explains that he was held by the Kartouf for a while but managed to escape.

"What was it that made the wound?" I ask.

"There was a bag," Lila translates. "A black bag. They pull it over your head and then tie it around your neck. They tie it so tightly it rips the skin. And it gets so hot it is hard to breathe. You think maybe you are going to die."

"How did you escape?" I ask him. He says they were moving him from one place to another but left the trunk ajar. When the car stopped for traffic he kicked it open and ran away.

"Were you tied up? Did you have the hood over you?"

Yes, he explains. But he managed to untie the knots, and the Kartouf members wouldn't chase him in a public spot. When he talks he keeps his eyes on his fingernails, which are thick, stained and broken, like most peasants'. It's hard to believe his story because so many young men claim exactly the same thing, especially the story of the trunk being left open. Peter has told me that if even a fraction of the tales were true there would be so many people escaping from open Kartouf trunks you'd be able to spot several a day on your own, just as you struggled through traffic.

"Mr. Punjo," I say. "Because we are an embassy, we cannot accept claims for asylum. If you want to ask for Canadian protection you must actually be in Canada. This is a long-standing international practice. Otherwise we'd be swamped and unable to operate the embassy. What I can do is refer your case to the International Committee for the Red Cross. They don't have an office here but look after this area from Manila. If I fax them this afternoon they might be able to send someone out within the next week or so, depending on their workload. If they find merit in your case they might be able to intercede on your behalf." When Lila translates he looks around as if he hasn't understood.

He asks where he should go now. She tells him that someone will contact him at the address he has given. He smiles strangely, though, when she says it, and then very seriously tells her that he can't go back to that address. Slowly, as if talking to children, he starts to tell us his story again. When Lila has explained the problem I tell him that he should contact us again in a week or so for an update.

He leaves, finally, but only with great reluctance, as if he hasn't understood.

The American Embassy is about a mile away, but we decide to walk since the traffic has been hideous the last few days. Peter says it's the worst he has seen it. Even at nine-thirty in the morning the sun is wickedly hot, so we walk on the shady side of Liberation Avenue, which has its share of mirrored skyscrapers providing almost a false front for a ramshackle marketplace just two blocks in. They're quite a contrast, these cool, modern, gleaming buildings and the dirty, seething, tired-looking stalls hunched to the ground, with customers pawing over the vegetables and chickens, the piles of fruit and plastic belts and knock-off radios, cheap shoes, nylon underwear, mass-produced imitations of Watabi art.

We consistently out-pace the stalled traffic. By the time we arrive we're sweating profusely. We show our cards at the gate and then are ushered into refrigerated splendour, a cool administrative palace bristling with clean-shaven security.

Greg Stevens meets us in the lobby. He's a trim, balding, affable man who says all the right things, even while his eyes quietly assess us and our situation. He's going back to the States on Tuesday, is happy to have a buyer who can pay in real currency. So in fifteen minutes it's done: I hand over my cheque, the Nissan is mine, the legalities are taken care of, and we're stuck in traffic on Liberation Avenue.

"It feels nice," I say, resting my hands on the leather of the steering wheel. "And the air conditioner really works!" So do the tape deck, the automatic door-lock and the electric windows. It's impossible, of course, to test the cruise control, inching along like this. But Peter has counseled me about being aggressive.

"Lean on your horn. If you're polite and let other people in you're never going to get anywhere. You'll run out of gas. That's something I forgot to check on. Open the trunk for me, will you?" He gets out of the car and rattles something before coming back.

"There's an extra container of gas in the back," he says. "In case you're stuck in traffic and run out."

I ask him about how the Americans could do all the paperwork for the transaction, including getting me a license, when I'd failed in three trips at the ministry.

"Sometimes they can really get things done here," Peter says. "Not always. Sometimes we can get things done better than they can, and sometimes nobody can get anything done. It depends on who you know and when you know them. But generally, yes, if anybody can penetrate the bureaucracy here it's the Americans. All that military money has to add up to something, after all."

"What do the Americans do when they want to get somewhere in traffic?" I ask.

"Nothing," Peter says. "They sit here just like the rest of us."

"I think we'll go up early with Marlene," Maryse says. She takes a bite of puffy toast and turns to call Patrick in from watching the spiders. "She's going up Friday morning and offered to give us a lift."

"Where'd she get a car?"

"There's an Australian one floating around."

"That would be okay," I say. "Maybe I could get off a little early, too."

"Oh, come off it." Maryse reaches her foot under the table to tickle between my legs.

"Patrick! Did you put your bug juice on?" she calls.

"Peter might let me go," I say. I eat a piece of *gundut*, a sweet white fruit with a hairy skin that peels easily.

"More likely there'll be some new crisis that you're indispensable for. This way at least Patrick and I will get to go."

Maryse is right, of course. At the office there's a crisis with the people from the Tulun Water Pump Project. Nearly fifteen thousand dollars of Canadian funding has disappeared, and Peter has me sit down with the director, Ruth Marjowi, to sort through the disaster of her files. Marjowi is a wizened, birdlike woman in her fifties, her nose curved as a raven's beak. She knows everyone in the development community and drops names throughout the morning, but she's useless at paperwork. We keep on through lunch, getting nowhere, and then I phone home but Maryse and Patrick have already left with Marlene. I promise myself that I'll leave by one, but it's closer to two-thirty by the time I finally gather all the files myself and tell Ruth that I'll take them with me to Kaireen and sort through them over the weekend.

"Maybe that's the best way to do it," she says. "It's so restful there. Everything becomes clearer."

"Yes. I've heard."

I stow my suitcase in the car and then remember I have to get the map from Peter, so I go back to the office and interrupt his meeting with two Australian Embassy people.

"Bill!" Peter says when I peek in. "Thank God you haven't left yet." And he stands and introduces me. "We've been looking for the quarterly visa stats," he says. "You haven't seen them?"

I have, and I find them, but I avoid sitting in on the rest of the meeting. Peter gets the map for me but doesn't have much time to explain.

"The green zones, right, are the safe areas," he says. "Stick to them, and make sure you have your ID, because there are a lot of checkpoints. And have a great time! Kaireen is fantastic. Just the ex-pats. Nobody else bothers with the trip."

In the car, finally, I relax a moment — change my shirt, put on my sandals, spread the map out on the passenger seat. I should go back to the office to take a leak, but I might never get out again. It's all right, I think. It won't be too long.

And it isn't. The cross-town traffic is freakishly sparse, so that I actually make it up to thirty kilometres per hour on Minitzh Boulevard, and an astounding forty-five kilometres per hour on the highway out of town. The checkpoints aren't so bad either. By now I'm used to mounted guns being trained on me and soldiers poring over my passport. "*Dijunta*," I tell them pointing to the word so they can't miss it. "Diplomat." At only one of the checkpoint stations do I get asked for money, and it's only 10,000 loros.

Then about a hundred metres past the seventh or eighth checkpoint, bad luck: my tire blows. I get out and notice how odd it feels to be alone on the road. I've broken down right next to a banana grove, and the mountains are close: brown and green against a sky strangely blue, now that I'm outside of town. The air doesn't feel that much cleaner but up in the mountains it must be better.

Luckily there's a spare tire in the trunk, along with a jack and tire iron. Stevens kept the car well provisioned: in the trunk, with the extra gas, there's a first-aid kit and a shovel. It's hot work in the sun and dust but it doesn't take too long to get the blown tire off. I'm so involved in the work I don't even notice the four men until they're almost beside me. When I look up I think they must have come from the checkpoint because it's the only place around. But they aren't wearing uniforms.

One of them addresses me in Kuantij and I say I don't understand. One more bolt and the spare tire will be on, I think. But at the same time I think, If they're trying to rob me I could drive off with the tire as it is.

If they're trying to rob me. I stand up but it's hard to know. They're crowding a little too close but don't seem hostile. I look back at the checkpoint. Nobody there, which is odd. No other cars, either.

All of the men are smaller than I am, but there are four of them and I'm not a fighter. Strange how these fleeting thoughts make the time seem much longer. One of the men, talking all the time, reaches to my arm. Not a hostile gesture, but I don't know what he wants. My wallet? I'll gladly give up my wallet. The car? That, too.

It's what I mean to do — surrender everything — and yet not what I do at all. I push the tire iron, which is still in my hand, against the arm of the man reaching toward me. It really isn't a violent movement, and yet because it's a tire iron I can't retreat. I drop it and lunge for the car door, slam it behind me and hit the autolock, locking all the doors at once. I turn the key and jam into gear, but I blow the clutch, the car leaps forward a few metres and then stalls. I curse, start the engine again, and turn just as the tire iron smashes at me through the window.

Shocking pain. Either the iron or a piece of glass gouges a cut across my forehead and the blood streams down into my eyes. The blow stuns me, snaps my head back. They open the door and pull me out. I try to fight, but they shove my face in the dirt and twist my arms behind me. Then the kicking starts, in my belly and ribs and groin. I can't breathe, can't get up, can't roll over or move. Eight, ten, twenty times it seems they kick, until I think if I just pretend to be dead they'll leave me in the ditch. I pretend, but they keep on kicking. They don't leave me anywhere. They tie my arms and legs and tape my mouth, then throw me like a sack of rocks into the trunk of the Nissan. It's too small, they have to twist my limbs to close the lid.

Don't take me! I think, but there's no way to call out, to escape. The pain in my ribs and stomach gets worse with every bump and jolt. Road dust fills the trunk and I think, I'm not going to survive this — I'm just going to choke to death. How to escape? What to do? It seems to take forever for a few simple thoughts to filter past the pain and the shock. It must be the Kartouf, I think. I'm tied in a trunk, kidnapped by the Kartouf, and all I have to do, if you believe the stories, is kick my way out. But this isn't a Kartouf car, this is my car, a Nissan. The trunk actually locks, and I can barely move my legs and feet anyway.

There's a black jumble of time, how long I can't say, until it occurs to me we're back in the city because the car is stopped or slowed most of the time and the temperature in the trunk rises until I nearly pass out. They might run out of gas, I think. They'll be stuck in traffic so long. They'll have to open the trunk to get the extra gas. That's when people escape from the Kartouf — in traffic, with other people watching. The authorities will notice the smashed window on a car with diplomatic plates. They'll know something is wrong. I have to stay alert for it.

If I stay alert, then in that one brief moment I can make my break. I struggle with my hands, try to loosen the rope. Any advantage I can get. Anything. People *do* escape from the Kartouf. All the time. Have to stay positive. If only I hadn't jammed the gears! I was almost away.

I work on my hands, work on them, until it almost seems as if the rope is loosening a bit. My left eye is filled with blood from my cut, but my right eye has stayed clear. If they were going to kill me they'd have done it right away. They're just going to hold me. To get a ransom, free some political prisoners, whatever. I have to hang on.

When the trunk opens finally I'm slow to move. My hands are loosened but the light shocks me, it's so sudden and bright. I sit up and the black thing moves so quickly I can't tell what it is, a rifle butt or a shovel. But it makes the pain split across my head for the slightest moment before everything is deep and still.

The video store is crowded for eleven o'clock at night, even if it is a Friday. Don't these people have things to do in the morning? If they're just choosing a movie now they won't be in bed before one a.m.

I don't have anything to do in the morning. There's a peculiar lightness to the feeling. My stomach is full of greasy, delicious crap that came in a cardboard box. I spent most of the evening lurking on questionable Internet chat groups, reading about other people's warped lives ("I recognized the smell of her cunt, but I couldn't recall her name"), went for a brief walk to clear my head, ended up here. It's a strange urban hunger, this lone-wolf bachelor feeling. Maryse has taken Patrick to Toronto to visit her mother and check out a gallery that might show her exhibit *Frog Dreams*, a multimedia re-interpretation of the frog prince fairy tale, but I have a reception tomorrow night at the Chinese Embassy. I handle videos Maryse wouldn't be caught dead watching: *91/2 Weeks*, *Basic Instinct*, *The Red Shoe Diaries*, tits and ass plus violence.

Which one?

48 Hours. A buddy movie. I remember seeing it before Maryse. There isn't a clear ten minutes without someone getting shot. Nearly every woman in the movie is either naked or walking around in her underwear. And Nick Nolte plays a violent, alcoholic loose-cannon slob cop with a gorgeous girlfriend who sticks around just for the sex. Great guy stuff.

I finally opt for *Blue Velvet*. Maryse and I went years ago at a repertory theatre but after only twenty minutes she turned to me and said, "Are you staying?" It was the first over-the-top scene, with the hero hiding in the closet while Dennis Hopper hyperventilates over the blue velvet girl. I said, "What?" and she said, "Oh, come on, you don't like this shit, do you?"

So we left. All right, it's shit, but it's artistically done. And it's just satire, you can tell by the ultra-brite colours in the opening shots, the flowers and picket fences, the fire truck going by in slow motion. To live in our culture you have to have some kind of stomach for violence, especially if it's been dressed up.

At home I clear away the refuse from dinner and settle. I watch with all the lights off — something else Maryse hates — the really awful scenes made slightly ridiculous on the small screen. Dennis Hopper isn't so in-your-face, the blue velvet girl seems more pathetic, not as sultry. But it's great myth-making, I think, this warped ride through the American psyche. When the fresh-faced hero makes love to the blue velvet girl and she switches gears, begs him to hit her, it becomes uncomfortably erotic, wild. I don't dislike it.

After the movie the house is silent, dark, cold. My head aches from fatigue and the strange hollowness of this time. Upstairs I turn on a lamp and sit at Maryse's desk in our bedroom, examine the things she has brought to this space: her grandmother's gold watch with the tiny hands, hanging off the side of her computer monitor; her painting of the two old barns at twilight with the sky so pink and purple; her photograph of Patrick standing under the umbrella; the burro's tail she inherited from her aunt that looks so soft and lovely on the window sill near the bed; her charcoal sketches of Patrick as a baby; her Thai earrings, the silver dangly ones, on the dresser; the poster from her exhibition, the lustrous green frog perched so calmly, like a set of male genitals, in the valley between the naked princess's legs.

The bedspread that Maryse bought at that flea market, where was it? In Almonte, maybe, that day she thought she was pregnant. Her silver hair brush from her mother, the fuzzy blanket she wraps herself in when her period is coming on and nothing else can warm her up.

Her old mirror, my broken belt, the bottle of oil by the bed.

Alone in the big bed, in the darkness, I rub myself against Maryse's silk camisole, but it's the blue velvet girl in my head, begging for it, begging.

My teeth clamp right through the flesh of my tongue. Body lifts off the table. Scream like the howl of a hurricane. Flesh burns from the inside. Try to turn to get away but the ropes. Scream and fucking scream. Everything shaken loose inside. Going to die. Any longer too long. Too long, too long, I'm going to fucking die! Try to reach my hands to rip the clamps away but can't reach, nothing can move. Next pulse worse, slams like an electric wall. Can't scream loud enough. Can't reach it!

Die! Die! I think. Please God! Only place for safety. But can't reach. He won't let me. Burning out my body and brain from inside but too slow. All the shrieking in the world can't take me out. Burning again and again and I yell out I'll fucking sign anything! But can't reach can't stop.

Pleading sobbing wailing shrieking. Stop it stop it stop it stop it *stop it!* But again and again. Teeth go through my tongue. Bloody mouth. I smell the fear and fire of it. Endless shriek cracks every nerve and bone.

Die, please God, let me let me let me please. But no release. Again and again. No way from now. Yelling, shrieking, writhing, but more and more and more. Stop it! *STOP IT!* Every shriek of fear and pain brings only more and more. Feet now, throat, nipples, fingers. Stuffing fire in my mouth. No. *NO!* Can't survive this. Can't. *Won't!* Kill me, please God, please!

Stop it stop it stop it stop it stop! I howl, as long as I can still form words.

Coughing, coughing, coughing.

"You aren't going to work today," Maryse says.

"I have to." Coughing coughing coughing.

I come down the stairs in my dressing gown and slippers, my brain soggy from the long night. There's a picture on the landing of Maryse as a child, standing trim and firm and strong in her swimsuit, her hair already a dark aureole, her bright eyes looking angels at her grandfather.

"Phone in sick," she says. She's feeding Patrick, who turns to smile at me, his face smeared with egg. In a shaft of sunlight his curls are translucent.

"I can't," I say, pausing at the bottom of the stairs. In her faded jeans and her worn, green sweater, Maryse's body is still trim and firm and strong, but her eyes aren't looking angels.

"What's it doing outside?" I ask.

"It's fine now, but it's going to be a blizzard this afternoon. Call them up and say you'll start tomorrow."

"I was sick yesterday," I say, as if that explains it. One or two sick days a year, that's fine. But two in a row and people know you're a loser. It's the department. Besides, there's lunch with Khoury. And all those bloody questions to answer.

"You have bronchitis!" she says, knowing it won't make a difference.

I feel better in the shower. I only have one coughing fit in the beginning, which ends when I spit up a gob of phlegm that swirls and swirls around the drain, hanging on as if it's made of glue.

I can't stay home today because it's my first day with the rapid response section, and Pierre is out with a bad back from a hockey accident, so there's no clerk available to postpone my questions. They're changing coordinators, so there's no one to make my excuses to anyway, and the questions are waiting, waiting, waiting. And there's Khoury. I don't want to miss the lunch. If I can make it through today then I'll be all right. I can put off some of the responses until next week, then take tomorrow off. I do have bronchitis. But I have to go in today.

"You're *not* wearing your raincoat!" Maryse says. We're in the front hallway now. "Come off it. It's minus twenty-two, Jesus" — she lowers her voice so that Patrick can't hear — "Jesus Christ, at least wear your parka. What are you thinking of?"

I change into the parka, then when Maryse goes to the bedroom to help Patrick with his broken alligator I change back into my raincoat and duck out the door. My parka has chocolate marks on the left shoulder from when I was carrying Patrick that time at the museum. I should have had it cleaned by now but I didn't. And Khoury is old guard — appearances count. I went with him to Beijing that one time before but got called home early because of Patrick's arrival. He has some say in who gets posted there. He knows I'm interested, but little details matter. I don't want to blow this.

The bus is late. I stand brittle in the wind, pulling the lapels of the thin coat around my neck and ears. I should have worn a scarf. I should have worn my parka. To hell with the chocolate marks. Khoury probably wouldn't even notice. I could run back to the house and rub them out quickly. I actually turn to do that but then the coughing takes me over, deep and rattling. The glue suddenly clogs my throat — I gasp and gasp, squat on the sidewalk holding my chest, coughing, coughing, coughing, until finally I can breathe again. A woman stops, stands over me, asks if I'm all right, and I half-rise, nodding, trying to make light of it, then start coughing again, worse this time. I hang onto the bus stop post and cough until the phlegm shoots out of my mouth and nose at the same time. Naturally I've forgotten to bring a handkerchief. I look around but the woman has moved on, and there's no choice — I wipe my nose on the sleeve of my raincoat. Then the bus pulls up. I shouldn't get on it. I should go back to bed. It would be so easy to do.

At 9:33 my computer melts down. I'm writing up my notes for a question on the treatment of homosexuals in China when all the letters on the page scramble as if fired apart by proton bombs. I sit stunned for a moment, bang several keys helplessly, then turn off the machine and fire it up again, only to read, in half a minute, SERIOUS DISK FAILURE WARNING 5703. I turn it off and leave a phone message with the misnamed Help Desk. As soon as I put down the phone I cough and cough and cough until my head is between my knees, my fingers gripping the sides of my desk.

I borrow a laptop from a colleague. The letters come up red on a tiny black screen so that I have to squint to read them. Worse, none of the macros are loaded onto it, so I spend forty minutes I don't have canvassing colleagues to find out which ones I need and then loading them. When they don't work I turn on my other computer again and read SERIOUS DISK FAILURE WARNING 5703. I leave another message with the Help Desk. Then I phone two hearings officers in Toronto, one in Calgary and one in Vancouver to ask them if their questions can be postponed. None of them is at his or her desk, of course — hearings officers are never at their desks. So I leave messages.

Every time I put down the phone I cough and cough and cough. A friend makes me throat tea and I burn my tongue, something I haven't done in so long it astonishes me. I turn to look at her like Patrick does when he suddenly bites his cheek at dinner, shock and pain before tears.

"Are you all right, Bill?" she asks.

"No, I'm not."

I'm not all right. I'm not all right. I shouldn't be here. I should be in bed with a hot compress on my chest, drinking clear liquids and eating chicken soup, thinking pure thoughts, resting, being served.

I put on my stupidly inadequate raincoat and get half-way out the building when Williams waves me down to tell me the lunch is cancelled.

"*What?*"

"Khoury's sick today. We're doing it next week."

I go out anyway to a local grocery, freezing on the way there and on the way back. Eat my packaged sandwich.

SERIOUS DISK FAILURE WARNING 5703. I turn off my computer and think about calling Maryse to come pick me up, but there's still a China question to get done today. I wash down my antibiotics with several spoonfuls of natural yogurt, which is supposed to help restore the bacteria in my stomach. I call New York.

"Freedom Association for China," comes the male voice, heavily accented.

"Yes, hello, this is Bill Burridge calling from Canadian Immigration in Ottawa."

"Yes?"

"I was hoping to get a statement from a spokesperson from your group. I'm doing background research for refugee hearings in Canada. I'm looking for a public, on-the-record statement that can be used as evidence. I'm afraid my question is very specific . . ."

"Yes?" comes the voice again, and I'm not sure he has understood.

"I'm looking for a description of prison conditions in a particular county in Fujian Province. It's called Changle County, near Fuzhou. Would you have anyone who can comment on prisons in that county in particular?"

"Yes?" comes the voice again, and I know he hasn't understood. I know too that it's a shot in the dark trying to get information this specific. So many of the questions are meant to trip up a sophisticated story, to test credibility.

"My Chinese pronunciation isn't good," I say. "I'm sorry about that. But would your organization have anyone who knows about prison conditions in Fujian province, particularly near Fuzhou . . ."

"People's Garment Factory Number 2 — in Changle County," he says, and for a moment I'm stunned.

"You know about this?" I ask.

"I was there — four and one-half year," he says slowly.

"The garment factory — is that a prison?"

"Exporting prison. For rehabilitation through labour," he says.

"And when were you there?"

"1987," he says. "Released 1991."

"And your name is — ?"

He tells me and I get him to repeat it, then spell it, and I write it out.

"Zhang Li, is that it?"

I'm so slow it's painful. He starts to tell me about the thirty prisoners per cell, all of them sleeping on the floor, wedged up against one another, having to turn over at the same time. While I take notes I look at his name again.

"I'm sorry," I say, interrupting him. "Did you say your name is Zhang Li?"

"Yes."

My heart's already pounding before I hear the answer.

"Mr. Zhang," I say. "I read your book just a couple of months ago. I had no idea you were in New York."

"Now in New York," he says, and I can feel the smile over the phone. Zhang Li! I can't believe it. A man who survived over twenty years in Chinese labour camps, from the Anti-Rightist Movement and the Cultural Revolution right into the nineties. And every time he got out he spoke up again.

"I had no idea you knew English," I say.

"Had a radio in Henan," he says. "Listened BBC every night."

Zhang Li! I almost call my colleagues over to the phone. Zhang Li. I think of the scene in his book during the famine in the early 1960s when he fought with two others over a frozen potato. He got the potato; the others died. The seven months of solitary confinement when his teeth fell out and he thought he'd gone mad. The manuscript that was smuggled to Hong Kong. I think of so many things and yet there hardly seems anything to say.

"How did you survive?" I blurt, regretting the question immediately.

"One thing after another," he says, and then, thoughtfully, "Not always best thing."

"To survive?"

"What you have to do."

I return him to my question about the prison camp in Changle County and he tells me about the industrial operation, the textiles for export, the system of administrative punishments, the two bowls of rice a day with meat once a month, and the big fuss that was made when they thought the Red Cross was coming for an inspection.

"Everybody — new clothes! Shower!" he says, laughing. How can this man laugh after all he has seen? "Then Red Cross no come — take away clothes, no more good food!"

"I'm sorry to have to ask you this," I say, "but was there torture, ill-treatment?"

"Electric cattle," he says, fumbling for the expression.

"Cattle prods?"

"Strap you down," he says. "Saw four men die — one month." He pauses, searching for a phrase. Finally he says, "Murdered. Cold and blooded."

I keep him talking, for selfish reasons it seems to me. Because I want to hear the voice of the famous prisoner. He sounds small, unheroic.

I keep wanting to ask him again, How did you endure it? What kept you going through all of the worst?

When I finally let him go I have a mass of notes. I rush down the hall to the library and flip through his book, *Solitary*. It only takes a moment to find the passage I remember:

> When I had sucked the last of the potato, and the cries of the two others were swallowed in the dust, I made a promise that I would kill myself as soon as I had the strength. I tried five times over the years. Yet the more I tried, the harder it became, until it seemed to simply be my fate to be dragged like battered steel through whatever life put before me. *I am here,* my

voice always seems to say, even when I have no voice left, when I would rather not be here. *I am here,* it seems to say.

On a colleague's computer I write up my information on the prison in Changle, wondering at how unlikely it was to find Zhang Li at the end of the phone line, to get a first-person account on such a narrow topic. As I work I cough fitfully, pushing myself, feeling a grim satisfaction for having forced myself to the office after all. At least I got to talk to Zhang Li! Yet in all this time, because of the work and because of the tinted windows, I haven't noticed the blizzard building outside. By the time I step out the glass doors it's inescapable. I run, hunched as if in a war zone, through the driving snow to the bus shelter, and wait there, stamping my feet and holding my chest, coughing, coughing, coughing, for over twenty minutes until finally the right bus arrives, crammed with office refugees, the aisles full and the windows steamed over. It's only when the doors open for me that I realize with horror that I'm carrying nothing but a twenty-dollar bill for a correct-change-only service.

Is this ride worth twenty bucks? I ask myself. It is, and I pay, and no one even notices. Slowly the bus moves into traffic and I worm my way back, the air reeking of wet wool.

Cold and blooded. Cold and blooded. It's how I feel, holding myself, hanging on. Just get me home. Let me sink into a hot bath. End this day.

I lose track of where the bus is going. The windows are so foggy, so many of us are jammed in. The man standing beside me is a street-person, in his sixties perhaps, in filthy clothes, his face smeared with dirt. When a seat comes open he motions to me and I take it even though he looks like he's in worse shape than I am. He moves to keep a distance from the other passengers, apparently to keep from dirtying their clothes. Finally he takes a seat near the back when there's enough room. His head slumps and his eyes close, and it's only then that I notice his construction boots and the yellow hard hat he's carrying in his hand. A young man in business clothes, about my age, says to him, "Tough day?"

"Man," the old guy says.

"You look like you've been working."

"Moving pavement stones," he says, turning his hands open to show how puffed and scarred they are.

"How do you stay warm working outside on a day like today?"

"You don't. You just keep moving," the old guy says. After a while he says, "Sometimes I wonder."

"I bet," the younger man says.

From the bus stop I battle every step home, leaning into the darkness and the biting snow, my gloved hands over my ears. When I get in the door I'm greeted by the warm smell of cooking, but the house is dark. I cough and cough and cough, shedding my wet coat. Maryse is lying very still on the sofa in the den, a blanket pulled over her, with Patrick playing quietly on the floor in the gloom.

"What's wrong?" I ask.

"Oh, honey," she says weakly. "I've got one of my migraines. It's been building all afternoon. I should have just gone to bed immediately but I waited. I'm sorry. Dinner's there."

Dinner's there, yes, but I have to go out shopping afterwards because there's no food left in the house, not a crust for breakfast. If I were a better husband I'd rub her scalp and neck and shoulders, would prepare a heat pad and a soothing drink and ask her what medicine she has taken. But I'm running so low myself. I bundle up Patrick and we drive through the blizzard to the mall where a handful of other unfortunate or misguided souls are wandering the supermarket aisles. Patrick rides in the cart and keeps up a patter all the way along.

"Daddy, why we are going shopping?"

"What?"

"Why we are going shopping!"

"To get some food for the next week. You see, here's the list that Mommy had put together."

"But why *we* are going shopping!"

"Oh — because Mommy's sick. Sicker than me, anyway."

"Mommy doesn't buy that!"

"What do you mean she doesn't buy it? Look, it's on the list — tofu."

"Not *that* tofu!"

"What difference could it make what kind of tofu I get?"

"But Mommy doesn't buy *that!*"

"Which one does she buy?"

"The orange one! Stupeo!"

"Who are you calling stupeo?"

"You, stupeo!"

I'm not a stupeo. But I have trouble locating the soya oil, and the corn starch is nowhere, and I stare at a shelf for four minutes before my eye finds the couscous. We go up and down certain aisles over and over, looking for the cereal, the salt, the peanut butter, the bread.

"No Daddy, not *that* one!" Patrick howls.

Loaded for the week, finally, my feet heavy, more coughing lurking in the back of my throat, I head for the checkout. It's close to closing time, Patrick is asleep in the cart, and few cash registers are open. As I pile my groceries onto the belt a man in his fifties appears behind me, his hands filled with tuna cans, his manner impatient and stressed. He keeps glaring at my week's worth of groceries and at the slow progress the cashier is making with the lady ahead of me. Still piling, I glance back at him and he looks away immediately. There *is* an express lane, I almost say to him, but he's eyeing it already, several lines away. It has perhaps ten people pressing in, all with their eight items or less.

Loading, coughing, looking back at this guy. It shouldn't bother me but it does at the end of this wretched day — his bad manners, his silent aggression. He wants to get ahead of me. He wants to push right in. He's too busy even for the express lane. At the end of everything else today, it's too much. I want to plant my feet, unload my cart deliberately, tell him to chill out, fuck off, go stick it somewhere. It's such a little thing, but it seems too much to bear. On the verge of coughing again, keeping my eye on the sleeping Patrick so he doesn't slump right out of the cart, on the lady ahead paying now, on this jerk behind me fidgeting, crowding, pressuring me.

"Excuse me," I say, turning to him. Then gently. "Would you like to go ahead of me?"

"Oh, would you mind?" he says.

"Not at all. I'm in no hurry," I say.

He squeezes by me and my relief is palpable, like water running off my shoulders. In his haste the man drops his tuna cans so the cashier has to bend down to pick them up, but she runs him through in a minute, and he thanks me profusely, again and again.

"Not at all," I say.

"Oh, what a cute boy," the cashier says, looking at Patrick, and she's extra friendly to me because of my gentleness. Slowly we bag the week's worth of food and talk about the bad weather and how close it is to closing time. On the way out, pushing my cart, I'm seized by an odd sense of the night's blackness pressed against the huge windows of the store.

There will be worse days than this, it occurs to me. Outside, I snuggle Patrick into the carseat and load the groceries into the trunk, then sit for a while in the quiet car, listening to the night.

"Daddy?" Patrick asks some time later. "Why we aren't going?"

"Did I tell you," I say, "I talked to Zhang Li this afternoon. Can you imagine it? I just picked up the phone and there he was."

I turn the key in the ignition but there's no sound. I check to see if I left the lights on, but I didn't.

"Daddy, why we aren't going?"

I turn back to look at him. The blackness around us is thick now, and suddenly I know — I don't know how but I do.

"Daddy, why you are crying?"

"The car isn't going to go," I say softly.

"Why not?"

I take off my mitt, reach back to hold his hand.

"The car isn't going to go," I say. "Your mother will pick you up."

"Why it won't go?" he asks.

"It just won't. I'm sorry. You'll have to go with your mother."

"Are you going to come, Daddy?"

"I have to stay here, I'm afraid." Dark, so black outside. Not like smoke, but a black blanket over everything, cold and still and too big to escape.

"You're going to go with your mother," I say, trying hard to find my voice, to sound convincing. "She'll need a lot of help from you. Do you understand?"

"No, Daddy," and his voice is thin, panicky.

"It's okay. It's all right," I say. "This is something my father said to me when I was little. Now I'm saying it to you. You have to have big shoulders."

"What?"

"So when the world is rotten you stand a little straighter. Let it wash off you like water. Bear up. Have big shoulders."

"Daddy — "

"It doesn't always work," I say. "But sometimes it's the best we can do. Remember this: nothing is lost. Especially not the good things. And I love you. More than anything. Will you wait with me?"

I look back through the blackness until it's hard to see his face anymore. There's just the tug of his tiny fingers around my failing grip. Then the room turns hot and airless again and I know there's no time left. After all this pain and waiting, when I want to la.. longer I can't. No soldiers are coming. No help.

The people who did this to me, I don't want any of them to escape. I want their bodies ripped flesh from bone. I don't want anyone to get away with this anywhere in the world.

I try to see something now but that part too is shutting down. The air slides into my lungs and out, in and out, until the sweetness of it is too much to bear, the sadness too much to hold.

"Daddy," Patrick says, his tiny grip slipping.

"You wait for your mother," I say.

"No."

"I'm telling you."

"No, Daddy," he says in that voice he gets when he won't back down and nothing can budge him from what he wants: a toy at the supermarket, to watch cartoons, no broccoli at dinner.

His Daddy.

"It isn't what you think," I tell him. "I have to go. I have no choice."

"No!"

No no no no no no no no no. No. He tightens his grip. It's pathetic. A flower against the steamroller.

"No, Daddy!" he says. Both of us reaching. It's coming closer. The darkness. I want to feel his hand so badly. You can't say no. He doesn't understand. When the darkness comes there's no choice.

"No," he says.

"Josef," I say, *linala* in my throat and mouth. Propped up at the table. Unshackled but shaking. Weak but not dead. Not yet.

"Josef, help me stand."

He looks across at me. He, too, has been defeated by this kidnapping. I see it now in the black circles, the weariness in his eyes. Stuck with me so long.

"I need to exercise. Help me stand."

At first he looks at me as if he doesn't understand. Why do they want me here? The question comes back to me for the first time in ages. Who's keeping me alive? Is it really Josef? Or is there an outside power? This must be taking far longer than they expected. Whatever it is they're trying to get. Somebody released. Elections. A ticket out.

It's taking much longer and they're afraid to kill me.

"Help me stand." I push my arms against the bamboo chair. Try to push my feet against the dirt floor. He just looks at me, astonished, as if I were about to go off a cliff flapping my arms.

"Help me stand!" I try to say it with the conviction of a weed splitting asphalt. I push against the chair, feel my body lift for a moment.

Josef doesn't move. The chair topples and I slump to the floor.

"Help me stand!" I grab for the chair leg. He knows I'm right. He knows I'm stronger now than I've ever been in my life. Muscles notwithstanding.

I prop myself on a shaking elbow, flex my legs suddenly. I know I can do it. There's life still. You can't stop it.

On one knee. Josef hasn't moved. Maybe he thinks I'm going to try to attack him.

The chair tilts over and I fall hard on my shoulder. Not like Patrick when he was learning to walk. No padding there. Just skeleton. Thank God there are no mirrors.

I reach, clutch the chair, pull it on its side closer to me. Hairy bugs on the floor. The strength of an insect. A fly in the water. Josef watching. Not moving.

The chair is more stable on its side. There's more to push against. But now I'm really sweating, out of breath. As if I'm near the end of a two-hundred-metre butterfly, that burning feeling in the legs and shoulders, wondering if there's enough air.

Pushing up. Trying to rise. Find my balance.

What's happened to my balance? I'm always supposed to have that. Riding the damn bicycle. I put in my time falling off. I learned walking before that. I shouldn't be back to square one.

I fall again, this time on the chair. Exhaustion, sudden and complete. My stomach heaves and my whole meal, clear and runny, comes back up, spills over the chair, the floor, my arm.

It's too much. Once again, like everything else. Tears wash down my face. It never seems to end, this moment. On and on and on. Trapped in the slowest murk of time. I was on the main river. I know it. Days were ripping by, I had a family, there was work, too much to do. Now it's a swamp in the loneliest back-water, where nothing moves and there's no way out.

Stuck in my own vomit, for the umpteenth time, I fall asleep.

I wake up in my little closet, but something has changed. I'm not shackled, there's no hood. I can see dull light under the door. And I can move my limbs. But oh — they're so sore! As if my attempts to stand were Olympian and now the muscles have turned to wood. My arm, leg, rib muscles all complaining, and yet it's the sweetest pain — the residue of effort. I sit up immediately, balance my back against the wall, strain with my legs — the pain again, worse but bearable. Pushing myself against the wall, rising, rising, until I slump back down. Rest now, catch my breath. Stretching my arms. Feeling the dirt of the floor, the rough rock of the wall, the yearning in my feet and legs and throat and chest to have my strength again. Like Samson quietly waiting for his hair to grow back. But I don't want to topple any pillars. Standing would be all right. Standing would be a start.

Push and balance, strain and lift, slump and relax. How many days pass like this? When I'm spent I collapse and sleep, and when I wake I try again. It's the oddest routine, and yet like some little channel that I'm digging with my fingers, with my own broken hands, it gets the water in the swamp moving a tiny bit. There's some purpose now to my breathing. I know the spot on the wall that I reached the time before, can push myself to it, hold it, hold it, before my legs buckle. Rest and sleep and try again. Little by little the muscles respond.

Linala with Josef and now some soaked bread that he brings, and sitting at the table I can feel the straightness of my back. Not strong, not yet, but getting stronger. When he opens the door and moves me to the table it's with a shoulder under my arm, an arm around my waist. Walking. My own feet pushing against the ground.

I begin to have wild dreams of escape. They're so exhilarating I can hardly wait to revisit them. In one I'm running through a meadow, my arms pumping, and there's a whole army of men chasing but they can't get me, their bullets miss, and the pleasure of simply running as fast as a body can is almost too much to contain. In another I have the power to dematerialize, to slip under the door like smoke and float softly off to look down on my captors from the ceiling. I hide so easily in the clouds from their fucking cigarettes.

"When I ged with Kartouf," Josef says, pushing bread toward me, "everything my family kilt and kilt. No thing leff. Just liddle bid my life."

He's in a talkative mood. It seems strange, but I think my slow recovery is opening him up.

"Juss lige you," he says. "Almoss death. Kartouf bring me

mountains, lives us like" — He looks around, wrestling for the word — "*Corrigos.*"

"Warriors?"

"Warriors!" He makes the word sound like *worriers.*

"You lived in the mountains?"

"All the rain season. No-thing for I-S to find you. Grow food, hunt, eed medicines. *Linala.* Tribal fude. Now you stronger. Ready go with us."

"Are you taking me to the mountains? Aren't we already in the mountains?"

"You ged stronger now. I see. *Linala* meg you stronger." He says something in Kuantij and I shake my head. He says it again.

"You want me to go with you to the mountains? You want me to join the Kartouf?"

"Jess like me. Nearly death. Then — join Kartouf."

"But I have my family still," I say. He looks at me, his eyes very sad, and I come close to throwing myself at him, my heart pounding. But I know it's a trick. He hasn't killed them. I heard Patrick's voice that time. On the television.

"In mountains," Josef says, puffing himself up. "Very strong!"

I nod, eat everything he serves me, listen as he stumbles again through his explanation. He's trying to tell me that I have nothing left. That I'm supposed to join the Kartouf. This is why I'm here. They've brought me down to nothing, are building me up again so that I'll join them and then the world will know the importance of their movement, the degradation of the Minitzh regime.

As he talks I nod, spooning down the food.

"Josef, where did you learn English?"

Blank.

"English — how did you learn?"

He makes a funny noise in his throat, which means he doesn't understand. I try several more times. Finally he nods excitedly.

"Inglees! Inglees!" he says and he gets up, leaves the room. For a moment I'm alone at the table, no shackles or hood. It almost feels as if they've left open the door of the cage, and yet I'm too scared to move. But Josef returns in a moment anyway, carrying a bundle wrapped in a colourful cloth. He sits at the table opposite me and unwraps an elaborately carved chess set with the strangest figures I've ever seen — two tribal groups, one in dark wood, one in light. The dark group seem to be headhunters — all the pawns are carrying skulls — while the light ones have just spears and small shields. Both groups have shamans for bishops, and their knights are water buffalos.

"Where did you get this, Josef?"

"Inglees!" he says, pointing to the pieces, then making a motion with his hands.

"You carved them?" I ask, making the same motion, and he nods. "Inglees Porter stay my family. All one rain. Ride us!" he says, making another motion — writing. I ask several questions, and gradually it becomes clear. Some Englishman named Porter stayed in his village, with his family, for one rainy season. Probably an anthropologist. But he brought a chess set and taught Josef how to play, and Josef got the idea of carving his own set of figures modelled on two local tribes.

"Play. Speak Inglees!" he says. The board is meticulously crafted, inlaid with polished squares of the black and light wood. He sets up the pieces quickly, motions me to play first.

It's such an odd thing, yet so familiar. The pieces are foreign, not the stylized European figures I remember, but hunched savages both more and less real. And sitting here in these ugly circumstances, suddenly playing a game for pleasure. Is this real? Or is this some vision my brain has cooked up?

I move tentatively, have trouble surveying the board, remembering what moves each player is allowed. Josef plays with rapid thrusts, not taking any time to think but reacting as if this were ping-pong. But his moves make sense. He keeps himself defended but his attacks come from all angles, led by the headhunters and the water buffalo, with the shamans spearing in and then the queen, an infant strapped to her back. I don't really know what I'm doing — it's been so long and the situaton is so strange — but somehow my tormented brain has kept an area reserved for this.

I lose a water buffalo stupidly, not noticing the danger, then a shaman in a forced exchange with a headhunter. Josef moves fiercely, his eyes bright.

"Where is your village?" I ask him, but he doesn't seem to hear. I ask again.

"No weel-age," he says.

"Where you carved these pieces?" I say. "Where is that village?"

"No anymore weel-age!" he says, and he makes a breaking motion with his hands. "Burn. No weel-age!"

"Your village was burned?"

"Every people," he says, and he makes a pistol gesture, his finger to his head. Pulls the trigger.

"Everyone was killed?"

He nods.

"But not you?"

"Almoss," he says, looking back at the board, moving impulsively. He's left himself exposed, so I take his castle — a thatched hut on posts — and he cries, "Aie!" his hand to his forehead.

Long ago hours ceased to have meaning, so I don't know if we last that long or if twenty minutes feels like a whole afternoon. But for a time it's such a relief to have something abstract and absorbing to focus on, something that has nothing to do with staying alive, with terror, with my hellish situation. It's just a game, a mock war. There, I lose my queen, but it's not serious — I can still fight. Josef gets over-anxious and I capture his queen with my remaining water buffalo. We're more or less evenly matched, and as play goes on I start to feel as if I can win this. I can win.

But it doesn't matter. It's just a game.

Josef stays on the attack even after he has lost his queen. I don't think he knows any other way. I try to stay safe, to counterpunch, wait for a mistake. He loses his castle on a risky move, then makes a blunder and loses the other one. On the board I have more pieces, I'm ahead, but he stays on me. I trap his shaman in the corner, take two of his pawns and then a third. The tide is turning and he knows it, but he keeps on attacking. Maybe it's his only way, having seen his whole village burned and murdered. The army, no doubt.

Clearly he's losing now, but it'll take many moves to hunt him down, and suddenly my energy drains away. I know I won't be able to focus. It will take too long. I don't have the strength to see this through.

There's no draw in Josef's brand of chess. It's death one way or the other. I can see that, as he starts to chop me down with the small army he has left. There's no draw, no resigning, no falling on your own sword.

And this is no game, really. Like everything else in Josef's world it's played to the death. It's a revelation, the pleasure of finding this distraction, the sorrow of seeing that it's no distraction at all, just another version of savagery. As he dismembers my resistance it occurs to me that I'm going to have to kill him. If I ever want to get out of here alive.

How to kill Josef? Days and days are taken up with this problem. I've lost count anyway in this backwater, things barely move. And yet change happens all the same. Pushing up against the wall, flexing. Then standing straight, on my own, barely wobbling.

How to kill Josef?

I think about it with the spoon in my hand. I could turn it around, jab the sharp end into his eye. Except that it would take great coordination, and there would only be one try, and even if I gouge his eye perfectly, so what? He turns, enraged, a thousand times stronger than me. Ploughs his fist through the cardboard of my ribs.

I could steal his knife. While he helps me back to my closet. I could reach around his waist, in one movement unsnap the leather holder, pull out the blade and sink it in the soft side of his belly. Over and over I go through the movement in my mind, practice in the darkness and solitude of my prison. When Josef pulls me out to eat I tremble with nervousness, realize as I'm walking with him that it's too far to reach, that I can't control my movements, am not strong enough.

Not yet. In my cell I lean my arms against the rock walls and push and push, Samsonlike. Flex my fingers, build my grip. Dynamic tension. Follow those comic book ads of my youth. Charles Atlas.

Collapse on the floor with weariness, sobbing with the pain and futility of it.

Here's the problem with getting a little bit of food after you've been starving: you're ravenous for more. My system has trouble with anything richer than the *linala*-soaked bread, and yet the possibility of getting more takes on enormous proportions. Josef can see me getting stronger, no longer helps me walk to the table. I gorge myself on mango now, a bowl of rice, papaya. Giddy with desire for more. Yet always conscious of the knife on Josef's belt. He must know what I'm thinking. I'm like a wild animal now, wounded, at my most dangerous. It's his fault. He's the one who awakened me. When I was near death there was lassitude. Nothing mattered. Nothing that was here and now.

And now everything matters. The feel of the spoon in my fingers, the texture of the food going down, the pain in my bowels of suddenly having to deal with this again.

He lets me piss and shit in a bucket by the table. Makes me do it after every meal. The stuff slides out of me on command. I grow aware of my own rank smell, of how filthy I am. Josef, too, has sunk slowly, is grubbier than in the early days, but not like me.

"I want to bathe," I tell him, and he just looks at me. "If you want to build me up, you have to let me wash."

He thinks about it for a moment. He's so goddamn lazy! This is what's behind so much of my ill-teatment. Not the torture, but the smaller indignities that have built up over time: the bad food, that rotten closet, the filth and degradation. He just can't be bothered.

"I need to bathe. Right now. Get me a tub. Water." I make a washing movement, pretending to scrub my face.

"No dub," he says, shaking his head. "No enough wader."

"You clean yourself," I say.

"No enough wader."

Sudden rage, almost overwhelming. I nearly fly at him, the bastard, the lazy fucking bastard, he can't even bring in a tub of water to help me bathe. It seems like the worst degradation, the last unendurable thing. And he sees how angry I am, starts to raise his hands as if he might need to defend himself.

And then I'm swamped with the certainty that I'm never getting out of here. Sobbing and sobbing, without shame, for everything that's occurred, everything that's been done to me. Taken away for nothing, for being unlucky, in the wrong place at the wrong time. Sobbing, too, for my weakness, for knowing there's nothing I can do against the Kartouf, against Josef. My pathetic little plans — injure him with a spoon, try to grab his knife! He'd break my bones like kindling.

Sobbing, sobbing, until I almost feel it's worth it to fly at him anyway, end it now, have him kill me. Not another minute like this. It's unendurable. Not another second. Because even if I survive it'll be with the knowledge that I did nothing — just accepted and suffered. That's who I am, the kind of person who allows this to happen to himself, who brings it on, does nothing to get out. What kind of life would that be? Spineless, haunted, trembling. Fighting nightmares every night. Shaking in the middle of the day, panicked at the slightest noise, losing my mind with the memory of it. End it now, I think. Better to have his fist go through me like cardboard than live as an insect.

It's a matter of timing. Josef comes toward me, his hands relaxed by his sides, his knife there on his belt. Just the one clasp. Slide it out and thrust immediately. Into the soft side of the belly.

He puts his hand on my shoulder. My face is streaked with tears, eyes blurry. Fast action, that's what I need, yet it's as if I've left my body, am trying to move underwater. I start to stand. This is my death, I think. This is how I die. Because, having endured so much, I gave up and threw it all away on a last gesture that was bound to fail. As I stand the chair pushes back and I'm aware of his body supporting mine. I look down and glimpse the knife. At the same time I think: I'm not going to do it, I'm never going to do it, this will go on forever, and: This is how I die, with this stupid final act.

Everything happens so slowly, then speeds into a blur. In a moment I'm dazed, on my backside at the other end of the room, not knowing what happened. There's no knife in my hand. I look around and after what seems an absurd amount of time I see Josef. He's not at the level I expect — instead he's on his knees, clutching his side, silent, his eyes bulging, tongue sticking out.

He rises to his feet somehow, face wax now, the blood spilling out as if from a ruptured wineskin. I expect him to turn on me, to pull out the knife and rip through my cardboard body. But instead he staggers from the room, blood trailing behind.

Shattered with fear and regret. Now I really am going to die — four or five other Kartouf will come rushing through the door and they won't be the civilized ones. I've already wounded the civilized one. The thought hammers through me and for a moment I'm paralysed with the instinct to go back into the closet and close the door. There'll be safety there. No blood. Everything fine!

Instead I lurch to the doorway, slip on the blood, get up, half-soaked. Into another room, expecting it to be full, an angry bee-hive. To face full attack! But it, too, is empty, except for Josef slumped by the stairs. He turns to me, clutching his side, pulls out the knife. Swears in Kuantij — there's no mistaking the tone. Why isn't he calling the others?

I don't have control over my body. Step goes after step in a weaving, jolting progress, my strength sapped before I even cross the room. But there's no other way. The others will be on me at once. But the harder I try the further away the exit seems to get. He has the knife out. He's dying but he wants to kill me first. I have to pass him. My heart racing, breath jagged. Fear! Fear and survival. The last locked coils inside me spring into action. He lunges and I pull his arm, roll his heavy body.

Now the others are on the stairs. Four of them race upon me, throw me back down with the force of an explosion. My head hits the floor and they come for me. I twist but it's hopeless. Two of them carry Josef to the middle of the room, lay him down gently. The other two drive me against the wall. Screaming, cursing, spitting. Choking me, hand so strong, the fingers nearly breaking my neck. Struggling but getting weaker. Going, going. Please let me go. Blackness . . .

Windpipe released. Gasping now, slumping to the floor, strong hands picking me up again. A pistol grip smashes me in the face. Try to raise my hands but they're held fast. Two, three, four more smashes. Blood now running into my eyes, mouth. Sobbing, pleading. Anything to not be here. Take it away. Make it a dream.

Bring me back to my cell. The hood again, shackles. Take it back.

The pistol goes right in my mouth. I taste the oil on the barrel, feel the electricty of shock and fear, taste it like burning rubber.

Screaming in my face in searing Kuantij. The others tending Josef, crying, some of them. The whole room pitched into disorder, anger, shock. I can feel bullets coming, explosion. I just know it with every fibre in me. This is it. The last breath. The last stupid moment.

I throw up. All down the barrel, on his hand and arm. It was so far down my throat. No choice. It catches him off-balance. He jerks his arm away, shakes the vomit so that it sprinkles into my face and down his grubby combat clothes. I know what he's going to do a second before he does it. He draws the pistol back to hit me in the face again

I can't stand it. Not there. It would hurt too much. Before he can move I kick the side of his knee as hard as I can. I don't know how I know where to kick or how I move so quickly. But I catch him square on the joint, and before he can smash me again his knee buckles sideways and cracks like a broken table leg. He falls over, clutching himself, and I bolt across the room. The others look up too late. I hear the pistol misfire behind me, then two shots smash the doorframe as I pass through.

Up the stairs. Flight after flight! Pounding footsteps behind me. What should take ten seconds lasts for hours, it seems. I keep waiting for a bullet to rip through my lungs. Know there's no way to escape them. Not when I'm so weak. Their hard breathing behind me. No more shots. Why? I turn when I know I shouldn't, and there is a sub-machine gun calmly levelled at my torso.

It has come down to this final stupidity. I watch him pull the trigger in slow motion, the burst of fire from the barrel. I can't even try to move. I see it from a distance, as if in a movie. As if I'm already dead. A line of bullets ripping diagonally across my torso, entering like needles, blowing out my back like comets.

Ripping the life from my body.

Blackness. Again. Waking from the deepest hallucination so far. Like coming from the bottom of the ocean, from the basement of someone else's soul. I'm going crazy. Can't tell anymore what's happening and what's fantasy. I want so desperately to be away. Anywhere. Anything different would be better.

When I see Josef again I stare at him, distrusting this reality. I've killed you already, I think. What is this strange place where the people you've killed are still alive and still your captors? When they kill you one moment but you open your eyes the next.

"Mountains soon," Josef says.

Drained, defeated.

"Soon rain. Then move. Ged strong!"

Linala in my bowl, some rice, a tiny slice of fatty meat. I eat in a disoriented silence. I can't sort out what's changing and what's staying the same. I look at Josef. I stabbed you, I think. I reached around and unbuckled your knife. It went right into the soft skin in the side of your belly. I saw the blood pour out. A lot of it got on me. I felt it soak my clothes.

I vomited on a pistol that was shoved straight up my throat.

"Eed! Ged strong!" Josef says.

Skipping like a rock over water, bouncing off now a flat surface, now a wave. Stretches of time in between that simply pass with no memory, no consciousness. I'm going crazy. Or I'm crazy already. I don't know what's real. I don't know anymore when I'm awake.

I have a strangely lucid dream of being borne on a stretcher, in the rain, at night, through the jungle. Up a steep slope made slick by the wet, the soaking leaves wiping against my face and body, the water pouring on me, soaking the rags I have left as clothing, chilling my skinny body. It's as intensely physical a sensation as when I thought I was running for my life up those endless stairs, when I turned and watched my body ripped with bullets.

Strapped in, helpless as cargo. The progress slow and laboured. There's a column of us, I can hear murmurs up ahead and in behind. Many bumps and lurches. The stabbing of branches from time to time, then halting on steep slopes, my feet much higher than my head while my porters struggle and strain, trying to get a purchase with their feet in the mud. I know now, from my last dream, that there's nothing I can or should do. This isn't real. If I close my eyes and drift then I'll wake up and this will be far away. Lying on the bottom of a canoe. On a lake, the storm coming up, black clouds heading this way. That odd feeling of floating just above the ground. My feet could touch but they don't want to. So slow, but effortless. Toward the camp where I saw Josef. In the jungle. With the fires and the dogs and the kids running. That camp from before. The weapons standing in a circle, black, ominous. So this is a dream. The same one from before. Part of that dream. But instead of looking at things from a height, from above, I see them from below. I'm flying much lower. And getting soaked. Shivering with the cold.

It doesn't feel the same at all. It must be real.

No. Nothing is real. Nothing anymore. It's all a dream. A nasty hallucination.

Or is this real and that other part — the part where I had a family, a career, a separate life — is that the illusion?

I don't care anymore. If they kill me. Or if I'm still in my cell or these are the mountains or really I'm dead and this madness is part of being a ghost.

Nothing matters, except it would be nice to be warmer, to have food, to be home.

"Rest now," says a kind voice, in a language I understand. It's daylight, though the chills make my teeth chatter. I open my eyes,
have been disoriented so long that it feels normal not to know
where I am, what reality this is.

It's Marlene, the vegetarian Australian. She's wiping my face
with a cool cloth. I'm lying on a bed of huge leaves, my head near
the low, rounded doorway of some sort of hut. The air smells
sweet and cool and vaguely smoky, all at the same time.

I don't ask right away what she's doing here. I assume she's part
of the splintered realities I can't understand, haven't understood
since my captivity.

"How are you, Bill?" she asks in a low, calm voice.

I just look at her. Since my death by machine gun I've resolved
not to participate in unreal scenarios.

"Can you talk?" she asks, wiping down my arms and hands. She
has such a loving, warm touch. I don't say a word, just watch.

"Nod your head, please, if you understand me," she says. I don't
move. It's part of the hallucination. To get me to believe, to act
again. Scare me shitless. It's part of my torture and I won't participate.

"I'm going to get you out. I heard through some contacts where
you were, and I've been talking to some of the right people. But it's
going to take a little time. Can you understand me?"

She peels back my rags, wipes my chest and belly. Tenderly, gin-
gerly.

"They've really done a job on you, haven't they?" she says, and
the sobbing nearly starts, I can feel my breath heaving, the shaking
in my shoulders.

"It's all right," she says, but I won't cry. I won't! I can't give in
again. It seems like my greatest act of will to push it all back down,
to regain control, to have no reaction, no feeling. I close my eyes,
wait for her to go away, for something else to replace her.

"Please listen, Bill," she says. "I can't stay long. I have some people to talk to before we can work things out. You have to hang on awhile longer. I've brought medicines and food. Josef has them. Make sure he gives them to you. He's a good man. I'll be back in a couple of days."

"What do they want?" I ask, forgetting everything, speaking up despite myself.

"Food for the villages," she says, "and an independent body to investigate the killings."

It takes awhile to digest the words.

"Whole villages are close to starvation," she says, "because the government is rooting out the Kartouf. They don't care how many are killed. The Kartouf wants them to stop, and it wants the story told. You got caught at the wrong time. They thought you were CIA. When they realized you're Canadian they didn't know what to do. That's all I've heard. Maryse and Patrick are fine. They went home eight months ago."

She doesn't ask how they've been treating me, if there's anything I need, anywhere special I've been broken or split. She can see already the state I'm in.

"Are you . . . part of the Kartouf?"

"I'm just trying to help people," she says.

She wipes down my legs, washes my feet with cool water from a basin beside her. Her face is suntanned and her skin clear, youthful, but her expression is hard. I don't need to look much past it to know how bad I am.

"Do you have malaria?" she asks, pulling something out of her bag. I tell her I think so, thought so at one point, don't know anymore. It comes out vague and garbled, as if I'm not in my right senses.

I'm not. I have to realize that. This could all be an illusion.

"I want you to take this medicine, one pill every morning. Do you understand?"

"They were giving me a needle," I say, trying to sit up. She holds her hand out, presses me back down. "I don't know when. They stopped."

"You're going to be all right," she says, in that way that really means she doesn't think so, probably not. They're polite words, leave-taking words, that I can't bear to hear. Even if this is just my broken imagination putting together faint hope.

It's something. More than I've had in a long time.

"If you hear helicopters," she says, "don't panic. It'll be doctors coming for you."

I grab onto her arm, and she knows without my saying anything. She can't go. Not right now. Not yet. Ghost or real, I need her.

The dream changes speed, keeps me off-balance. Heats up the air around and inside me so I feel as if I'm immersed in water slowly coming to a boil. But the rains come again with whipping winds, and the water washes through the camp. Literally. At one point I reach my hand out from where I'm lying and feel a stream of cold water surging past, carrying twigs and leaves. I catch glimpses of children outside the hut, banana leaves over their heads as umbrellas. They're cold, soaked, skinny children, shoeless, in clothes tattered as mine. Cheerless, somber, luckless children, sometimes massed together to hunt for rats. Flashing machetes, with vine whips and bamboo rods. A few women, too, their eyes large but listless, looking at me but past me. I'm a ghost anyway. An immobile ghost.

There's food sometimes, a thin soup, some boiled roots, once in a while bits of mouldy flat bread. A kind of bitter tea that rakes my throat as it goes down. Is this the food that Marlene brought? If she was ever here. I never see when it arrives or when the plate is taken away. That seems to be part of my life as a ghost. There are vivid moments of this reality but they don't last long. I'm suddenly launched into my eighth birthday party and then fiddling with my tie in Graham's room on my wedding day. Sheets of rain streaking the windows, the wind whipping up the dresses of the bridesmaids. Feeling in my pockets for the car keys, trying to make a getaway after the ceremony. Where are they? Looking up at the grey clouds and seeing Josef standing over me, the rain dripping off his mustache. His arms and shoulders so thin. Thinking: why are you at my wedding, Josef? Why aren't you dressed properly?

I have a speech to give. Where is my speech? It was in my pocket, too. With the keys. My keys are gone and now so is my speech, so how am I going to get us out of here and what am I supposed to say? I remember writing it out so I wouldn't forget. But I can't remember what I meant to say!

And Josef is no help, either. He's gone now, too. Everyone goes. It's what I'm beginning to understand. No matter who you think is here — Josef, or Marlene the vegetarian Australian — they go away. Everyone does. If you want something then you have to get up and get it yourself. Especially when it's raining on your wedding day. When you've lost your keys so you can't get away and you've lost your speech so you can't remember what you thought you wanted to say. Something loving and funny. And short. Something like that.

I get up but it's hard in these clothes, which aren't my wedding clothes at all. Christ! Everything's gone wrong! Where's Graham? He was organizing everything. Now I've lost my keys and my speech and I haven't even got the right clothes. There was the tuxedo from the rental place. Gentleman Squire. It's due back tomorrow. But I have to wear it first before I can take it back!

So hard to walk in the rain. Maryse is going to be so upset. She wanted this to be perfect. Had pitched battles with her mother over the arrangements. There were supposed to be pictures in the garden.

Where's the garden? The rain has washed away all the flowers. This is a disaster! This isn't just a rain but a typhoon. Little pathways turned to roaring streams, carrying away the garden. It's hard to avoid stepping in them. I lurch to the right but feel lightheaded. Why did I drink so much? I was so stupid. Losing my keys, my speech, my bloody tux. How am I supposed to get us out of here?

A woman stares at me from a hiding spot in the bush, a cave dug into the undergrowth. Is she part of the grounds crew? Or she's a neighbour, maybe. She's staring at me as if I'm the crazy one.

I try to check my watch to see if I'm late or if there's time for the rain to let up. But I can't find my watch. Everything's gone to hell! I can't believe it. Everything I touch is screwed up. Maryse will be furious. She'll whip her engagement ring right back in my face. How could I forget my watch? Without my watch I'll never know what time the ceremony is supposed to start. I'm trying to remember. What did I do when I got up this morning? I can't even remember that. I must be losing my mind.

Then Josef is pulling at my arm, yelling at me in a foreign language. He isn't dressed yet, either. What's going on? How could he come to my wedding in such miserable clothes?

Yelling and yelling, but the rain's too loud. We can't have a wedding in this. I don't care if all the arrangements have been made. This is awful. The wind now whipping the trees ferociously, twigs and branches hitting our faces.

Suddenly Josef flies from me, he can't hold on anymore. His body twisting. He lies still. Stunned, I just stand there for some moments before I see the helicopters.

Why are there helicopters at my wedding? It doesn't make sense. The guests suddenly run out from their hiding places, some of them screaming, twisting, falling the way Josef did. Who did we invite who would arrive by helicopter?

Marlene screams at me from a gushing dirt-track stream near the edge of the little clearing. The wind is so loud I can't quite hear. What's she talking about? And why isn't she dressed? I don't know why Maryse invited her — we've hardly known her for very long.

A little boy right in front of me grabs his hip suddenly, twists and falls face-first into the mud and water. When I reach him his body comes apart in my hands — his left leg falls off when I turn him to get his face out of danger.

Marlene runs toward me. She has a big girl's awkward stride, seems heavy on her feet compared to the others around us, so tiny, forest people almost, wild and thin and grubby. Marlene makes a strange progress toward me. She runs several strides, turns to yell at the two helicopters, whirling right at the edge of the clearing, their mounted guns flash out in the rain. Marlene yells, then turns to run at me some more, then turns again when an old man a few metres away gets blown apart. Why is this happening? I can't seem to move or react but just stay where I am in the open. None of it makes sense.

Two soldiers in green leap from the helicopters and race toward me, machine guns in their hands. They start well behind Marlene, but because of the strange way she runs, her stopping and starting, they quickly outdistance her. It's as if my feet are planted. I know the right strategy for this hallucination. Don't participate. They can't touch you if you stay still. That's the truth. It's taken me so long to learn it. When you start believing and participating, that's when you get scared shitless. When you're open to being crushed. It isn't real if you don't allow it. I know that. I know.

From behind one of the huts to my left there's an explosion and one of the two soldiers running at me is suddenly airborne and screaming. He lands across the clearing on jagged rocks that catch his body in a strange grip. The other soldier is blown backwards, too, but keeps his feet. Both helicopters turn at the same time to rake the hut and surrounding bushes with machine gun fire. The leaves and branches wither in seconds and a child of about ten raises his head for the briefest time, then collapses into the underbrush.

You see, I almost say. It's better to stay very still. They can't touch you then. No matter where you're standing. Don't participate. Don't give in.

Marlene and the soldier reach me at the same time, just as one of the helicopters starts to move toward us. She's screaming abuse now, right into his face, and the helicopter sweeps up behind us like something prehistoric and sinister. I suddenly want to run and yet my feet stayed rooted. Don't give in, I think. It isn't real. None of it's real. If you just wait then the illusion will change into something else and something else again. I've seen Josef killed before. I killed him myself, and he came back, strong as ever.

I've seen this before but Marlene hasn't. She strikes out at the soldier and just then the gun in the helicopter lets loose and her body jerks forward and back at the same time. "Wait!" I scream, but that makes it much worse, I'm plunged into it. It isn't real until you allow it, but once you do you can't claw your way back. The soldier smashes the butt of his weapon into my chest, bowling me backwards, then slings me up and into the helicopter, which blows with the wind and the rain of a hurricane. When we rise above the clearing the machine gun is still strafing, and Marlene's body becomes something tiny and twisted below me. Though she's wrapped in mud, I think I can still see her mouth open in anger, her eyes staring us down.

In the darkness I blink my eyes to make sure they're open. It's hard to tell sometimes — I get so still that I forget. It isn't really darkness. Not the darkness I've known. There are many shades of grey. On the far wall, for instance, mottled areas where the moonlight from outside penetrates the venetian blinds, and the barest hint of light from the hall has crept under the door, reflects off myriad surfaces. Slight, but there. Not dead. I can see all the shades, come down almost to their own little dots. They aren't static either but dancing, alive with their own rhythm.

Peter asleep on the low stuffed chair by the foot of the bed. It's hard to see him from this angle — the hospital bed is so high, the chair so low, the light so weak. But I can hear his breathing. He's grown a moustache since I saw him before. Thick and brown, it makes him look ten years older. He has been by my side since the helicopter landed. My guardian angel. Through the meetings with Santa Irenian IS, with CIA, with CSIS, the telephone call from the Prime Minister. The poking and prodding of doctors. Negotiating, arguing, yelling, interpreting. Soothing, coercing, deflecting, convincing. Keeping them off. Acting as shield.

I haven't said a word. Not since Marlene was killed. They got me that time. I participated, and look what happened. So I won't anymore. I'll keep my eyes open, but it isn't me, I'm not the one. I'm not in it, just watching. Dreams happen, there's nothing you can do but stay outside. It isn't real. When you close your eyes and open them again everything changes.

The tall American, the one with the huge jaw and the little eyes. Robinson. His neck too big for his collar. Bearing down on me.

"What we want to know, Bill, is what they did to you. I know it was awful, but we want to be able to counteract it. We want to get inside their heads. What you've been through, what you know, is a valuable weapon against them. Believe me, you *want* to use it. You *want* to fire back at them. You've got the weapon in your hands right now. You have to use it. You've *got* to tell us."

His voice like water rounding a bend, but with a steady, driving pulse. Easing you over that tricky part. Going on and on. Trying to turn your head.

"Was it electroshocks, Bill? I don't even need you to say any-thing, just turn your head one way or the other. Left is Yes, right is No. Okay, Bill? You still have the marks on your body, so we know already. But just to confirm — was it a black box sort of thing, like a car battery? Is that what they used?"

"Roger — "

"Excuse me, Peter, I'm trying to establish a connection here."

"We agreed this was going to be completely voluntary, but I don't see Bill volunteering."

"This man has just gone through hell of a variety we want to learn about!" His big face turned full on Peter now. "If he doesn't pass on his information then the whole experience has been wasted. He might as well have snuffed it months ago."

"Roger — "

"Can you understand that, Bill?" His big face on me again. "Silence is what these people want from you! They wanted you ei-ther dead or doing what you're doing now, hiding down in your hole. Are you going to let them do that to you?"

Just looking at him. Still as a lizard. It's what I learned. Don't give anything away.

"You *beat* them. They had all the weapons, you had *no* chance, and you beat them anyway. You stuck it out. Now what are you going to do with that? Just throw it away? Or are you going to help us learn from this?"

Just looking and looking till the scene changes, everything goes away.

"Roger — give us some time." Peter stepping in, putting his hand on that massive shoulder. It goes away. Everything does. Is replaced by something else.

The Santa Irenian Minister for Internal Security. Such small hands. Smelling of cologne, cheeks puffy, kept his weak eyes off me. His adviser had the hard eyes that registered and stayed fixed. Tightened his jaw. Thinking what? It could have been him. What would he have done? Checked out early. Been shot up trying to tear out someone's eyes. Like a warrior. Not a fucking civilian.

No questions from these gentlemen. They knew already what they needed to know. Better me than them. Better that they exterminate the Kartouf than end up broken like me.

"From Government of Santa Irene I would like expressing from hearts of all the people our sorrow and gratitude to you, Mr. Burridge. You are true hero just like in American movies, and from you we learn courage and desire to stay on with our everlasting struggle against terrorism. We say to you our deepest respect for your sufferings and promising vigilance of eternity to root out and destroy Kartouf terrorists as our government's main priority. Thanks God to you Bill Burridge, and godspeed you and your family."

The minister reading from a little card. The adviser's eyes never leaving mine.

Now in the gloom I watch Peter. I can imagine the time he's had. Dealing with the press, the department, cabinet. My family, the Santa Irenian government, the IS. Pressing for action, for news, for some kind of solution. Human rights groups, military people, diplomats, lobbyists. Trying to save a friend and colleague. His own career. Now that I'm out, am safe, he's not going to let anything slip again.

It could have been reversed, I think. Peter could have been kidnapped, and I would have been the one back in the office handling the crisis. It would have been a professional matter then. A learning experience. *Burridge on Santa Irene. His first posting and he had to handle a kidnapping—his supervisor, for God's sake. Played out over months and months. You should have seen the fellow when they finally brought him out. Like the walking dead. Couldn't utter a word. Burridge running around handling everything. Cut his teeth on a real crisis first time out.*

Cut his teeth. Instead I had my teeth smashed out. Barely

made it alive. Should have died, I think. Have no right being here. Traded my life for Marlene's.

"Peter," I say, in the gloom, the first slow signs of dawn tinting the room. He doesn't wake up at first. I have to clear my throat, get rid of the mucous that has collected like rust. "Peter," I say again.

He rouses slowly, shakes himself, tries to focus his eyes.

"Peter."

He comes to my side.

"What is it, Bill?"

"I want to go home."

He clasps my hand, closing his eyes briefly, the tears running so swiftly.

"I'm going to bring you home, Bill," he says, weeping. "But you can't travel just yet. We have to build you up. The plane trip is very long."

"I know that," I say. "But — I've been through worse."

Both of us crying now. No way to stop. Floods and floods.

"I'll set it up," he says.

"Mrs. Brown," I say into the telephone. Peter has cranked up my bed. Daylight outside. More rain. "Mrs. Brown, I'm sorry I couldn't come to the funeral. I owe my life to your daughter, and I just wanted to tell you — how sorry I am that I couldn't come and that — "

The words stop there, running out as if falling over a cliff. My hands start trembling and Peter has to hold the phone for me.

"It's nice of you to call, Mr. Burridge," she says, her voice low, words careful.

"What she did — " I say, but again the words fail. I shouldn't have tried this. I can't go through with it. There's nothing I can do to lessen the blow.

"The Santa Irenians have been very kind," she says, after a pause. "There were some officials who came. They told us everything about how it happened." Pausing to breathe, breathe, breathe. "And they promised they'd hunt down the Kartouf killers who shot her."

"The Kartouf?"

"Yes. Well, you were there," she says shortly. Then she says, "We've had so many faxes and letters from around the world. It's been wonderful. It really has. And I got a card from your wife. They were such good friends. She and our Marlene — "

Choking and sobbing on the other end. I've just made everything worse. I shouldn't have called.

"Mrs. Brown, I'm so sorry!"

"It wasn't your fault!"

I can't bring myself to say any more. It's Peter who eases us out of the conversation, who adds his own regrets, the gratitude of the people of Canada. I can hardly think for the sound in my head of Marlene yelling at those soldiers. The villagers getting shot up. Marlene's body all shot up. Not by the Kartouf. By the government soldiers.

Everything slipping away now, changing like water, disappearing and re-appearing as something else.

"Let's go, Bill," Peter says gently. I'm dressed now and sitting on the edge of the bed, staring at the bare wall. I've waited and waited for this moment, and now that it's here I'm no longer sure. I've felt so safe in this room. Finally. Why should I change?

I try to walk down the hall but last only a few metres, climb into the wheelchair puffing, my heart hammering, sweat running like rain. I must be eighty years old.

Peter signs the register, talks briefly with the nurse in Kuantij. When she comes over and kisses my cheek I tighten my jaw. Something's wrong. I don't know what it is. But things are happening too smoothly. The two Santa Irenian military guards walk smugly beside us. It isn't right.

A crowd of photographers at the front entrance. We go out the back way, sneak around behind them so they don't even notice us. Peter helps me into a little car, one guard squeezes in beside us, the other gets in front. Someone else I don't know driving.

It isn't right. I know as soon as I get in. It's a set-up. Avoiding the photographers. Going this back way. Who's this driver? A young guy, scruffy in the face although his clothes are clean and pressed. It's just like the Kartouf to get only some of the details right. And these guards, looking out the window so calmly. Why? Because they know it's a set-up. Because they've been paid off. Just like the guards at that road-block who knew when to disappear.

Fuck it! I can't believe I'm sitting here, trapped. Peter on my left, an innocent. They'll take him too. What a coup! Recapturing Burridge and the other Canadian official supposed to be protecting him. It's a perfect operation for them, to show the country that they're still strong.

Stay calm. What to do? The guard beside me is wearing a pistol. It's in a shoulder holster right by my elbow. I give it a sidelong glance. Try to measure the distance. I'd have to grab with my left hand and transfer it to my right. Fiddle to find the safety. I don't know anything about pistols. But just having it in my hand could make a difference.

We pull out into traffic. The guard in front motions me to keep my head low so the photographers won't see me. But I want people to see me, to be known. I don't want to fucking disappear again.

"I think he wants you to slouch down," Peter says. I turn, nearly yell at him for that. But have to keep control. He doesn't know. He doesn't have a clue what the situation is.

"I know what he wants," I say in anger. Peter is puzzled. Figure it out, I think. Put two and two together.

I breathe, breathe, try to stay calm. We glide by the photographers. Nobody sees. I almost yell out. Almost grab for the door.

My heart going boom boom boom. I've been here before, know better what's happening. The driver checking in his mirror, stepping on the gas so aggressively, leaning on his horn. It's sunny now but was raining earlier in the day, so the roads are awash with puddles. The hidden potholes don't stop the drivers from darting maniacally in and out, until the traffic is twisted and clogged. Of course. This is Santa Irene, the island paradise.

The guards seem unconcerned. They're professionals all right. They know what's coming down. I'm stuck in the middle of this little anonymous car, in the middle of this wasteland of stalled vehicles, in the middle of the sorry capital of this miserable country. Pinned, squeezed, secured. The Kartouf squad could arrive at any moment, could just run right over the tops of four lanes of cars. In a flash I realize they wouldn't want to kidnap us. That didn't work the last time. They would just take us out. Give the driver and the guards ten seconds to get clear.

Peter sits beside me, oblivious. Looks at his watch. Unconcerned. He planned for traffic, left plenty of time. But we're never going to make it. We're not supposed to. It's going to happen at any minute.

Not if I can help it. I've lasted through too much to get caught now. I could burst through on Peter's side. Would have to unlock his door first. One motion. Like with Josef that time. When I got his knife and stabbed him. He wasn't paying attention. You can surprise anyone. It's worth more than strength.

My heart hammering while I work out the details. Have to stay calm. Can't tip them off. Without surprise I'm useless.

"Are you okay, Bill?" Peter asks. I glare at him. He just doesn't know. He doesn't have a clue.

"We've got plenty of time," he says, putting his hand on my arm. "Don't worry. It's just Santa Irenian traffic. Do you want a drink?" He pulls open his bag and hands me a bottle of water. The driver and the guards turn to look at me. The driver lights a cigarette. Alarm bells clang in my head.

It's a fucking trap! No way to tell Peter without tipping off the other three. *The whole country's a fucking trap!*

We stay stuck in the traffic. I sip the water, waiting to hear the boots charging over the tops of the cars. Closing in. I never do anything. That's my problem. I just stay trapped where I am, waiting for whatever's going to happen. Suffering, enduring. I can't any more. I know that. My nerves are gone.

Have to act. Like that time with Josef. I got his knife. I just did it. Ripped it through him. At least it was something. It wasn't waiting around. I did get his knife. He didn't know what hit him. Wasn't expecting an attack from a cripple.

But it didn't really happen, I tell myself, my heart still hammering, breath shallow. Fear grips me. I hate this. I hate it! Not knowing. Being stuck here. Exposed and vulnerable.

I never got Josef's knife. I only imagined it. I never tried, and so Marlene was shot up. It was my fault. And now if I stay here Peter's going to be shot up, too. I'm half-dead anyway. Peter doesn't even know. He thinks these people are bringing us to the airport. He's lived here four years and he doesn't know!

I reach for the guard's pistol. Just suddenly do it. Stab out with my left hand, but I'm in such a state I come nowhere close. The water bottle spills down his lap and he turns to look at me in alarm. "Bill!" Peter says. I try some more for the pistol but don't know where I'm grabbing — my hands just slap out uselessly. The guard pushes me off. Peter wraps his arms around me from behind. I struggle for a moment then fall limp, gasping and crying. They've no idea. They none of them have any idea!

"It's all right! Bill — it's okay!" Peter says over and over, holding me, calming me, while I just try to breathe, to keep things together.

The medication helps. On the plane I slip in and out of dreams. Flying sometimes, but snakes, too. They seem far away. Everything seems far away. I have that feeling again of being outside myself, not trusting what seems to be happening. It's better that way. All these feelings, these alternate realities. No way to decide among them. They're just set up to make you suffer. Like walking down a sidewalk and stepping into a hole big enough for you to crack your shinbone.

Why did I think of that? The slippery Santa Irenian sidewalks after a rain. Worse than ice, those tiles. You think you're okay but you aren't.

Peter sits beside me reading. The world's largest ocean below us, under a platform of clouds. The plane drones while I sit still as a lizard.

Remembering her voice on the phone, so strange and distant, brittle.

"Bill? Is that you? Are you all right?"

"Yes. I'm okay. I am." Lies and more lies. She'll shatter when she sees me, I know. I wouldn't let her come to me, hoping that I'd recover somewhat before she saw me. I'm sure she's seen the pictures on the TV and in the newspapers, will try to prepare herself. But there's no way to do it, really. I've lost decades.

The plane forever droning, a pointless battle it seems against vast distances, to be in this little room high above the world. Yet this is familiar. To sit still as a lizard, feel the breath slide in and out, as if that in itself could be entertainment. Watch the time drip by. It's not so bad, sliding in and out of different states. Dream and awake. Watch the clouds slowly, slowly changing beneath us.

Droning, droning, time slowed down. It's how everything has been. And from this place, still as a lizard, as a rock beneath a lizard, I feel as if my whole life has been lived and re-lived. Is that a silver lining? To know how easily life is crushed. And yet have those coils push right back up. Come pavement, winter, death, disease. Starvation, disappointment, the rot of age, chalky bones. The memory of light and human touch. It's never enough. You always want more. Even when you've been driven crazy.

Finally, when forever is over, the plane banks and heads down through the clouds for the last time. Peter grasps my hand and I try to smile for him. He really has been with me every moment.

"Are you ready?" he asks.

"Yes," I lie, suddenly dreading this new reality. It would've been easier to have died almost anywhere along the way.

The flight attendant unfolds my wheelchair and she and Peter lift me in. Before I leave she asks for my autograph and I'm stuck, pen in hand, trying to remember what my signature looks like. Finally my hand moves and produces two large Bs with some jagged squiggles between them. The marks of a crazy man.

Wheeling out of the aircraft now, down the chute and along the tunneled passageways. A short, middle-aged man in uniform bows his head suddenly in recognition, straightens and salutes as I pass. The press, getting the story four-fifths wrong, has made me out some sort of hero. I was helpless the whole way through. Lucked out in the end. Got Marlene killed. Have died myself a dozen times.

Emerge now a wreck of a man.

Suddenly a crowd surges in front of me. Peter raises his hands but is engulfed by flashing cameras, TV lights. Microphones, questions yelled at me. "How does it feel to be back in Canada? Do you believe the Santa Irenian government will be able to eradicate the Kartouf? Is it true that the Kartouf used government torture methods? How did you survive?"

"Ladies, gentlemen, please!" Peter shouts, waving his hands — my protector. "There's a press conference scheduled for ten o'clock tomorrow morning. Mr. Burridge is exhausted from the long flight and from his ordeal. He will not answer any questions now."

A team of government officials surrounds me like blockers in a football game. Calling instructions. Peter wheels me hard left, then jogs, pushing me, while the journalists follow in a swarm. We plunge through a set of doors into a darkened lounge. The reporters pound the door, trapped outside.

Two people in the shadows by the padded bar. Two lovely people. Maryse carrying herself so straight, breathing so carefully, as if she has forgotten how. Her hair completely white now — shockingly, made old at a stroke. And so I know. But her face still so smooth, so apparently young. Not turning away. Even from the horror of her husband. And Patrick, so much bigger than I remember, running straight at me, his face lit, so that I have to stand, I can't let him see me any other way. He grabs my legs and I hug him awkwardly from above. Want to lift him to me but can't.

I'm here, I want to say. On my feet. Not in a box. It's something.

Everything, in fact.

But no words escape. So hard just to breathe, to keep control.

Others emerge from the shadows. My parents, crying, and Graham and his wife, holding a baby I've never met. We none of us know what to do or say, and the moment gets stuck like a bone in the throat.

But if you breathe and breathe and breathe the next moment comes. It always does.

We go back to the apartment Maryse has taken downtown, the second floor of an old house. It's strange to see our old furniture shoehorned into these small rooms in different combinations from what I remember. There are clusters of conversation in the kitchen and the tiny living room, with people looking at me but not looking, close to tears but not crying. I stand for a while then sit, yammer away saying anything that comes into my head, then subside into a silence that feels like the bottom of a landslide. I'm pinned limb to limb by a ton of rocks, little rocks, big rocks, pressing down on every inch of me, couldn't move if I wanted to. Couldn't talk, think, get up, breathe. Pressed flat but somehow still alive. The hubbub lasts through dinner, and then Maryse sends them all away. I pull out enough to thank them, to hold them, but they don't want to feel my frailty for too long. This is not body to body but body to bone, and they aren't comfortable embracing skeletons. Nobody would be. Too much to ask.

When they're gone there's a deep and near-panic silence which I try to escape by pleading fatigue. For a moment I worry that Maryse will want me to sleep with her in our old bed, but she explains there's a single bed in the guest bedroom, and could I sleep there at least for a while? Patrick has been climbing into bed with her at night so she can be with him when his nightmares start. She's a bit embarrassed — I used to take a hard line on Patrick sleeping in his own bed. I remember it while she's talking, like something I read.

"No, it's fine, it's perfect," I say, relieved. "I'm not . . ."

"It'll take some time to get your strength back," she says.

She walks with me to the bedroom, holding my arm like I'm the eighty-year-old father and she the middle-aged daughter. I sit on the bed and she pulls my old pajamas from the dresser and lays them beside me. For a moment I think she'll try to undo my shoes and undress me, but instead she stands.

"Well. I'll leave you to it," she says, stumbling for the right tone. Then she turns, blessedly closing the door. She doesn't want to have to see my body. The wreck she's married to. I don't blame her. I'm glad she doesn't. I don't want her to see.

Once in bed I lie on my back with my eyes wide open. Every moment ticking by. It could be eternity. The unchanging pattern of the shadows. Breath going in and out, relentlessly, stupidly. Me watching it all. There will be no sleep. Not for me. Man of bone. I had a thousand years of sleep. I'm all slept out. Finished my quota. Will not have a peaceful night's oblivion the rest of my life. It's completely obvious.

Their voices are broadcast into my room. Perfect reception. Patrick so big now, sounding so grown up. Chattering with his mom while he takes off his clothes for his bath. "Is Dad going to get his teeth back?"

"We'll bring him to the dentist," Maryse says gently. "When he's feeling stronger."

"Grampa keeps his teeth in a jar at night."

"Yes," Maryse says, trying to be bright. "It'll be something like that."

"He *will* be better," Patrick says. Trying to convince himself.

Maryse says, "There are some other things. Your dad has problems with his insides. Because they treated him so badly. I'll be bringing him to the doctor's quite often in the beginning, I'm afraid. But they can do wonderful things."

I don't hear Patrick's reply. They go on to talk about kindergarten, about a project, about some show he wants to watch. Easy, flowing, carefree talk. This life they've built together. Because I was gone.

After they go to bed the shadows deepen and I watch the digital clock turn over. 11:20. 12:31. 1:05. 2:31. Odd moments of precise, meaningless time. Lost at sea time, undifferentiated. It could be anywhere. This is the ugly part. I could be back in captivity. Lying here. It's no different. The bed so soft it's uncomfortable. Me immobile, heart hammering, the minutes ticking over, not ticking, stalled. It's all right, I tell myself. But it isn't all right. There's no escape. No escape! You can fly halfway around the world and surround yourself with friendly faces, but at night there's no escape. Close your eyes or not.

I get up suddenly, step out of the room, try to calm my breathing. Fumble through the shadows. I spent so much time in darkness my eyes should be like a cat's but they aren't, are worse than they were. The malnutrition, I think.

Glasses, false teeth, physio, drugs. We can rebuild you. I stumble through the kitchen, opening drawers. Not my kitchen. Everything strange. Trying to be quiet. Trying. Then I sit in an old chair I remember. In the living room, by the window looking out on the street. The shadowed part between the street lights. This chair was in my parents' house. Stuffed and green, with springs that squeak. But I can sit in it still as a rock beneath a lizard. I remember it from earliest boyhood. I used to curl up in this chair with my blanket, even before Graham was born. It was the safe place.

The light changes slowly with the passing of the hours. My heart goes hammer hammer hammer but still I can see the slight changes. In the dark there are molecules of light, I can see them. Small, fuzzy, blurry little grains that get bigger, start to spread into unstable patterns. One thing flowing into the next. I think about it and think about it, holding the edge against myself, watching the blurry little grains.

"Couldn't sleep?" Her voice startles me but it's all internal, a shock wave within. I turn my head slowly. See her in her long T-shirt. She approaches from behind, passes a warm hand across my bony shoulders, squeezes briefly. Then sits on the sofa a few feet away, tucking her legs under her in a feline-female motion. Blurry there in the gloom.

"Must be jet lag," I say, with some clumsiness. All this need to explain.

"Yes. It'll take awhile." She looks out the window. Nearly dawn. The grey is lightening suddenly. "I feel as if I haven't slept since they took you. I tried these industrial-strength drugs that knocked me out cold, but I never woke up feeling I'd been asleep. My mind was on the case all the time. I had to leave the island. I'm sorry. I really couldn't stand it."

"It's what I wanted," I say, my voice cracking.

"I . . . I took to praying," she says. "I hope you don't mind. I actually found myself going to church. We met a very nice group of people there. Very loving and supportive. Patrick and I both have been going."

"That's wonderful," I say. Still as a rock beneath a lizard, my voice coming from somewhere far away. "I found myself hating God," I say, "this slimy little voice deep in my cells. Keeping me alive through all that shit."

"Oh, Bill, I'm so sorry," she says, crying but not moving toward me. She has a tissue in her hand in a second, and then I notice them — tissue boxes scattered throughout the room.

"There's a . . . well, it's a kind of therapy group that meets at the church," she says when she's regained her voice.

"In the daycare," I say. "In the basement."

"How do you know?"

Hammering, hammering, hammering.

"We sit in these little chairs," I say. "There's a group of us."

"Bill?"

"Only I could never remember the social worker's name. There was Linga, a Tamil, and a Sikh gentleman, and a Chinese lady, and Luis Gomez. Dr. Gomez."

"What are you talking about?"

"It was God. That slimy little shit. Showing me that whatever they did to me, I wasn't going to escape. I was going to have to live through it. And it'll always be there. To happen again and again and again."

"Bill — " she says again, but urgently this time, and then she sees through the shadows and reaches across in a flash. *What did you do?* " but she knows it all immediately, grabs the paring knife and throws it across the room. "Oh my God, oh my God!" she cries, pressing my wrists. They're quite wet. Everything, all of a sudden, is quite wet. Surprising amount of blood for a man of bone. Then she runs to the phone and I hear her punching in the numbers, but she doesn't realize. It happens so fast. After so much slow time. She races back to me with the roll of tape and the sirens sound right away, as if they were waiting just around the corner. Knew this would happen. Knew it!

On the stretcher as they wheel me out, the light so suddenly bright. Dawn. The gaping, awful possibilities of it. Maryse's face so full of shock and hurt. I'm sorry. *I'm sorry!* But she doesn't understand: there's no escape for me. I lived through the reaches of hell and will live through this, too, because I'm a slimy little shit, spineless and unredeemed. I'm going to have to suffer the false teeth and the physiotherapy, the nameless social worker pressing her pencil to her clipboard: "And how did it feel when they did that? What did they do to you next? Then what?"

The doors of the ambulance now closed, the illusion of speeding away down the street, of heading toward safety and peace.